Exile, or, A Tale of Enchantment in Eight Parts

T. Edward Abbott

Tiny Boar Books   Port Townsend, WA   2021

Tiny Boar Books
Water Street
Port Townsend, WA 98368
www.tinyboarbooks.com

The Library of Congress has catalogued this edition as follows:
    Abbott, T. Edward
    Exile, or, a tale of enchantment in eight parts / T. Edward
Abbott -1st Tiny Boar Books ed.
        1. Magical Realism—Fiction. 2. Fairy Tales, Folk Tales,
Legends & Mythology—Fiction. 3. Horror—Fiction.
Library of Congress Control Number: 2021907302

ISBN-13: 978-1-955290-03-6 (paperback)

Titles by T. Edward Abbott

On the Nature of Things

The Crow Foretells a Stormy Day

Exile, or A Tale of Enchantment in Eight Parts

T. Edward Abbott

Exile

IV

Contents

FLOOD

IT was odd that she should be wearing sunglasses in his office. At least, so Adrian thought. Flashing half-circles, each just large enough to obscure one pale eye. Reflecting the glare of his desk lamp back at him.

Especially, he mused, observing her as she leant against his rusting, leukocyte-green filing cabinet, given that his office let in no natural light. Like the office of every other functionary at his pay grade, Adrian's faced the atrium. His single regulation window did nothing more than filter the chilly illumination of the LED sconces that lit the ground-floor food court into his line of sight. And ordinarily, he kept the blind closed—the blue of the LEDs clashing with the yellow from the desk lamp that he needed to keep from weeping as he worked. Processing visas. The blind was closed now. People thought him antisocial.

Not that he minded. The lack of an exterior view, that is. (Though he also didn't mind being thought anti-social.) For security reasons, few of the offices in the behemoth structure faced outward. Windows were an unacceptable defensive vulnerability, and windows for every dispensable entry-level officer would have been a laughable proposition. Even the Consul General, whose space on the top floor did present a view— or, so he had heard; Adrian had never ventured beyond the third floor—looked mostly at the backs of the heads of the Marines, nervous, tense, and scattered across the ramparts, protecting him.

All of which left her sunglasses a mystery to him. Though, he rationalized to himself as he carefully filled in the form in front of him, she wore them everywhere else in the Consulate as well. His office wasn't an exception. Even if he did wish she spent less time visiting him, in particular. He wasn't sufficiently important to merit her monitoring. Her interest made him nervous.

He kept his head bent down. His eyes averted. Slowly, very slowly, writing.

Five years earlier, Adrian had completed a degree in Comparative Literature to much acclaim and to enthusiastic predictions of academic greatness. And then, three days after receiving his diploma, he had shocked and dismayed both his family and his teachers by joining the Diplomatic Corps as a flunky. On a whim. Because he'd stumbled across the application at midnight, online. Possibly he'd been drunk.

His mother had cried. His dissertation supervisor had derided him as a clerk. And Adrian, uncertain as to why he'd taken the step— except, perhaps, to provoke tears in his mother and undignified umbrage in his dissertation supervisor—had ignored both, curious if not excited to see where his decision would take him. As it happened, his decision had taken him to the decrepit Republic in which he now resided.

Admittedly, he'd been disappointed. An unadventurous type—travel in and of itself was not his interest; he'd travelled sufficiently with his family and, later, for his graduate program to satisfy himself that the world was much the same everywhere—he'd hoped for Paris. At a stretch, Florence. When he'd been informed of his posting, however, he'd taken it in stride. At least he'd been assigned to the Consulate rather than to the Embassy.

For though the city in which Adrian now lived had once been the capital of the Republic, it had been downgraded a century before to nothing more than a thriving commercial center, when the founder of said Republic had deposed and slaughtered what had been the country's ruling monarchical family. The founder—"Our Great Founder," according to official history—had then erected a new capital city on the site of an abandoned monarchist village (well, "abandoned") in the middle of a frigid and infertile plateau five hundred miles to the east of the original capital. Security, he'd familiarly argued. The new capital city could be defended against attack in a way that the old city, riddled with remnants of the ancient regime, could not. Not to mention that it was more hygienic.

Adrian would have wilted on the plateau. If
nothing else, he'd have been unable to shrug off
the commanding gaze aimed at him from all sides
by the still proliferating monuments to Our Great
Founder—monuments that glowered down on
pedestrians from nearly every street corner. He
flicked his eyes up at the blinding circles
concealing the eyes of the woman watching him
from across his office. Not unlike her gaze, come
to think of it. Tradition was to leave out the pupils
in artistic representations of the founder. Adrian
wasn't yet comfortable enough with his contacts in
the Republic to ask why.

Though the old city that was home to the
Consulate was refreshingly free of vigilant stone
avatars of Our Great Founder, however, Adrian
had nonetheless experienced a second
disappointment upon his arrival in the country.
He'd assumed, upon a quick read of the history of
the region, that Consular duties were undertaken
in what had once been his own nation's Embassy.
A charming belle-époque structure that had been
built upon the smoldering remains of an earlier
edifice that had burned to the ground when the
then-ambassador had challenged his Russian
counterpart to a drinking contest involving the
country's famed fermented goat's-milk spirits. The
louche "foreign" neighborhood in which the
Embassy-turned-Consulate stood, globally
celebrated for its drug and bondage culture, made
the seedier parts of Paris seem conventional by

4

comparison. Adrian had been looking forward to sampling it.

But by the time Adrian himself had arrived in the Republic, the old building had been abandoned by his native government—sold to a neighboring monarch whose family had fared better during the troubles at the beginning of the previous century, but who then found himself in need of a holding pen for his drug-and-bondage obsessed nephew. And the secure, state-of-the-art fortress in which Adrian now labored had been established in a suburb eight miles to the north. Adrian himself had never visited the belle-époque edifice. Not wanting to depress himself more than he already habitually was.

The suburb in which the new Consulate had arisen was abandoned. Or, that is to say, it was and had been abandoned in the same way that the monarchist village that had given way to the Republic's capital city was and had been abandoned. And indeed, Adrian's government adhered to the fiction of virgin ground with the same easy tenacity that the Republic's official historians had. Its opening had been celebrated with much subdued fanfare. A little over a year before Adrian's arrival.

No one knew what had happened to the non-existent people who had lived in the area before his government had purchased the land. They'd vanished. No evidence. And in their (nonexistent) place had surged triumphantly upward a remarkable facsimile of the mildly fascist architecture characteristic of the capital city on the plateau: surrounded by the same blighted, infertile miles of fencing wire; embedded in the same easily-defended nothingness; very clean and very, very hygienic.

In a gesture of respect to the country in which they were guests, the designers of the Consulate had even erected a statue (though less prodigious than was the norm) of Our Great Founder shaking anachronistic hands with the bewigged and comparatively dainty founder of Adrian's own Republic. The eyes of neither had pupils. And the somber, sculpted group gave Adrian a chronologically dissonant headache whenever he passed it to enter the building. He tried not to look in its direction at all.

Once more, he risked a glance across at the woman's sunglasses. He'd just finished—as slowly as he could manage—the form on which he'd been pretending to labor since she'd entered his office. Soon, he'd be forced to interact with her. Frowning, he moved his pen, painstakingly, across the numbered boxes. Grateful, as he frequently was when prominent members of the Consulate's staff sought his company, that this particular form had yet to be digitized. Most were still completed in hard-copy triplicate. Plausible deniability. Physical things, unlike digital things, can be lost.

It was possible, he supposed, wrinkling his forehead at a small blot of ink on his index finger, that his confusion about—and manifest distaste for—the new Consular building had itself first drawn her attention to him. A stupid error, but he'd been unaware of its repercussions during his initial months in the city. Indeed, far from keeping his disappointment to himself, Adrian had vocally expressed it to several of the other officers of his pay grade with whom he was encouraged to socialize. Sufficiently aberrant behavior at least to raise eyebrows—and yes, perhaps also to invite scrutiny. For while they'd gamely and piously voiced their gratitude for the safety and security of the new arrangement, Adrian had scoffed. When they'd said "terrorism," he'd laughed.

Certainly, he'd remarked, finishing off a glass of the local spirit, the Republic was unfriendly to their own government. Few countries weren't. But terrorism? The last significant terrorist event in the city had been when partisans representing a neighboring breakaway state that had failed for three hundred years to gain independence from the empire to the north that had always ruled it had occupied the local Four Seasons Hotel. The occupation had lasted for two and half hours, after which, satisfied by an interview on the state-run news network and a crate of the hotel's beer, famously brewed on-site, they'd decamped.

A few months later, five of them had formed a boy band, and two of their singles were still topping the regional charts. There was talk of Eurovision. Hardly an impetus to razing a suburb, erecting a fortress, and quadrupling the Marine presence surrounding it, Adrian had jeered. And his fellow entry-level officers had gazed at him across the sticky taverna table with solemn, fishy eyes, before encouraging him to drink a few more glasses of the fermented goat's milk.

After having lived in the city for a few additional months, Adrian had come to recognize his earlier callowness. One didn't question security. One certainly didn't mock it. Instead, one appreciated the fencing wire, and one felt a quiet and upstanding relief at the great distance between oneself and the **BDSM** clubs that flourished in the interior bits of the old city. One did not venture out trying to catch a glimpse of the nephew of the non-deposed monarch.

Screwing the cap back onto his pen—a resentful gift from his father upon setting out on his adventure—Adrian folded his hands on his desk and smiled politely across at the woman. Elaine. It was also possible, he eventually allowed himself to admit, that she simply sought him out for his education. Rumor had it that she'd taught for over a decade at one of the more rarefied universities back home before taking up her position here. Adrian couldn't imagine why she'd have thrown over the wood paneling of her previous institution for the flickering **LED** lights of the fortress—but then, few, including himself, could understand his own similar decision. They were, in a grotesque sort of way, kindred spirits.

Nonetheless, he didn't trust her. The familiar quality of her intelligence left him in equal parts exhausted and frightened rather than open and cordial. Not to mention that no one could tell him

8

what her role at the Consulate was. Her official title was "Economic Affairs Liaison," but even Adrian knew that meant nothing. His entry-level colleagues—at least, those few who hadn't discarded him as a lost cause—also whispered phrases like "talent spotter." Which left Adrian even colder. He had no talent. The literature he'd once compared was written in languages that had nothing to do with the region. He emphatically did not want to be spotted. He also wished she'd remove the horrible sunglasses.

"I've come with a proposition." She remained standing. Disregarding the chair he'd offered her.

"Oh?"

Perhaps this, now, was the spotting. If so, he was pleased, because he'd finally be in a position to demonstrate to her his utter lack of interest. Until she made him the offer, he couldn't very well reject it. And he'd felt for over a year now that said offer, ominous and undesirable, was always imminent, always just on the verge of realization. She held it over him, inching it in his direction, whenever they met. It raised his hackles. Which she seemed to enjoy.

She smiled, reading his expression. Though her eyes were concealed, the furrows surrounding her mouth were prominent. Strong, yellow teeth. Adrian believed she was a year or two shy of sixty. A long and frightening career.

Quiet and still, she didn't respond to his empty monosyllable. Patient. Expectant. Trick of her trade, he presumed. But he wasn't going to let her goad him.

"What proposition?" he eventually clarified.

She pushed her hands into the pockets of her bulky, unfashionable jacket. The top part of a skirt suit that looked as though it had been rescued from the wardrobe of an American actor playing a mid-twentieth-century East German interrogator.

"Have you met Callie?" she asked.

Not what he'd been expecting. "I don't think so."

He tried to keep the impatience from his voice. Though Elaine certainly didn't deserve it. "Who's Callie?"

"The Consul General's daughter."

"Oh." He had no notion of where the conversation was heading. He waited.

"She's been unhappy recently," Elaine persisted. "Since her father's appointment, really. Hoping for Paris, I believe." She tossed him the same unreadable smile.

"Oh," he repeated. He was beginning to understand now. But he didn't want to understand, and he refused unequivocally to accept the conclusion he was drawing. The woman couldn't possibly expect him to—

"She's a literary girl," Elaine pressed on. "Intellectual. But also sweet."

He gaped at her. Disbelieving.

"Close to your age, too."

He shook his head. All that kept him sane upon departing the Consulate every evening was his personal time in the city. Divorcing himself from the hellish daylight hours he'd passed in the fortress. He'd taken recently to visiting an archaeological site that had only weeks before begun yielding striking artifacts—stone statuettes, humanoid divinities of some sort. A local student attached to the dig had even allowed him to handle one. The woman couldn't *possibly*—

"Anyway, the Consul General himself has reserved the *Oppenheimer* for you both tonight." She removed the sunglasses for a moment, but Adrian still couldn't see her eyes because she merely ran a thumb and index finger over her eyelids before replacing the glasses. "It'll be waiting for you at the dock downtown at 6:00. Callie will meet you there. Don't eat. The crew will serve dinner on board."

He gawped at her. Unable to understand why she would do this to him. Aside from sheer, unmitigated malice. Sadism.

"No need to thank me."

"What?"

"I suggested you to the Consul General myself." She was turning toward his door. "A great career opportunity for you."

As she left his office, she paused and twisted back. The lamplight still glinting off the lenses of her sunglasses. "Oh, and Adrian? If you'd stop by my office sometime early next week, there's another issue I'd like to discuss with you. Don't worry about making an appointment. I'll free up time for you whenever it's convenient."

And she was gone.

Adrian stared down at the useless form on the desktop. A visa application. Denied. They were always denied. Another error he'd made early on in his time at the Consulate: carefully evaluating each application on its merits rather than according to its origin. Only the applications that came to him by hand, personally, from individuals known to the Consular staff, demanded his consideration. The others, the formal requests, were rejected as a matter of course. He slipped the form into his outbox. Still not yet digital. Easily emptied, and then lost.

After that, he stood to retrieve his own jacket from the hook on the door. Elaine had obviously organized this lunatic evening as some kind of arcane test. And he, Adrian, meant to fail that test. Spectacularly. If he'd wanted a great career opportunity, he'd have remained in academia. All he sought from the Diplomatic Corps was privacy, peace, and perhaps a small, entertaining bit of Kafkaesque nonsense. A place to age in harmless invisibility. Unlike his flamboyant and destructive father. About whom Adrian never, ever thought. Including right now.

Instead, glancing at his watch and buttoning his jacket, he stepped out of his office and onto the open gallery overlooking the food court. Callie and the *Oppenheimer* would be expecting him at 6:00. More than enough time between now and then to visit the archaeological site. Absorb sufficient strength and stamina from its stark beauty to survive the evening. Secure something in a mental compartment to cling to as he boarded and endured the boat. He pushed all but the little stone figures from his mind and made his way to the stairs.

THE *Oppenheimer* was a small, underpowered, mid-century teak powerboat that was owned by the Consulate and that navigated the waterway cutting the Republic's second city in two. Incapable of moving at more than eight knots—and four when going against the current—the boat trundled up and down the length of the channel, to the great delight of visiting government dignitaries and entry-level staff alike. Flying the flags of Adrian's homeland, it was an odd sight when it ventured out onto the choppy waves. Oblivious, or so it seemed, to the impression it was making.

For the waterway, a longstanding source of international tension, was a serious bit of geography. Connecting a major inland sea shared by the Republic and three frequently warring nation-states to a series of the more prominent global shipping lanes, it was also the only outlet to the ocean of the looming empire to the north that continued to think of those same belligerent nation-states as its territory. Their populations having been more fortunate—if only just—in their bids for independence than those whose representatives had taken over The Four Seasons.

As a result, the ferry traffic that joined the two sides of the city battled eternally with the massive tankers and the almost equally massive warships that day and night made quiet claim to dominance over the purportedly international channel. And the *Oppenheimer*, its flags waving, bobbed about in the wake of these leviathans like a steamboat skippered by an animated rodent chugging its way through the Battle of Okinawa. It was, to all who witnessed it, a bewildering spectacle to behold.

Adrian, who had of necessity enjoyed voyages on the boat more than once, had always been baffled by the apparent popularity among his colleagues of jaunts on the *Oppenheimer*. Unable to understand how the same people who believed that their personal security at work demanded a windowless fortress surrounded by miles of checkpoints and fencing wire were perfectly pleased to frolic open and exposed on a cheery toy boat that could hardly have been a more tempting target had it been painted to resemble a duck. He himself frequently felt the urge to blow it up. And Adrian's tendencies toward terrorism were minimal at best.

Though, admittedly, as he approached now with the sun sinking behind the far shore throwing Callie's frail form into relief, the boat did ominous equally well. When called upon—as it was currently. He wondered, as he involuntarily slowed, what Elaine had planned for him. Certain that it was something more than an awkward dinner engagement—even as he remained indignantly dumbfounded as to what he'd ever done to her to attract her notice in the first place.

14

Callie, from the little gossip that he could remember, was a lesbian. Which Elaine knew as well as he did.

Clutching to his chest the plastic sack he'd brought with him from the dig, he forced himself to approach the gently wobbling boat. The sack's contents would see him through the evening, he told himself. If necessary, he'd focus only on the sack's contents. Talismanic. Palliative. Helping him to compartmentalize.

Because what Adrian transported in the sack was, he felt, truly a treasure. A discovery beyond all expectation. A collection to savor while lingering over his remarkable luck and, ideally, forgetting Callie and the *Oppenheimer* altogether.

He'd come across it, the contents of the sack, that afternoon, in the following manner:

Having driven his Consular-issued Fiat directly from the office to the dig—omitting even to change out of his suit—Adrian had expected little from the hour or two he'd spend there before his obligation down at the docks. When he'd arrived, however, the student he'd befriended had appeared uncharacteristically jubilant. Charged—even from a distance.

Beckoning Adrian toward a newly excavated trench, more eager than his usual mordant irony allowed, the man had even grinned. A facial expression universally acknowledged to be a trait of Adrian's own Republic, rather than of the one in which he currently resided. Adrian had never before seen the man's teeth.

15

Adrian, surprised but not overly interested, had slammed shut the Fiat's door, loosened and removed his tie, and then—stuffing the tie into his pocket—trotted over to the trench. Where he'd seen, perfectly preserved, fifty-three of the little statuettes lined up side-by-side, staring at him. As though, for thousands of years, they'd been waiting. Hungering after precisely this moment.

His friend, once more in the trench, had used a tiny brush to expose the face of the one closest to Adrian. Allowing its eyes to find Adrian's. And Adrian's eyes to lock onto its own. An uncannily insistent face, Adrian had thought at the time, despite the stylized features. A face that knew its desires—and that acted upon them.

After climbing up out of the trench, Adrian's friend had clapped him across the shoulders and led him to an ice chest full of bottled water that sweated, isolated, under a makeshift tent. Tossing one bottle to Adrian, he'd grabbed another for himself and drunk a little more than half of it in three swallows. Before soaking up the perspiration on his own face with a crumpled bandana he'd pulled from a buttoned pocket.

"Those little goblins are going to turn this place into the next Sutton Hoo," he'd announced, finishing off the bottle and tossing it onto a collapsible table also protected by the sunshade. "And I'm the new Heinrich Schliemann."

Adrian had blinked at the chaotic references. And then, taking a small sip from his own bottle, he'd been unable to resist responding with

16

something baiting. "Isn't your government still angry with Heinrich Schliemann?"

"Nope." His friend's grin had turned manic. "Not after this." He'd slapped his chest. "Now *I'm* Heinrich Schliemann."

Adrian had laughed, and then, pleased by the success of the dig and his friend's happiness, he'd led the man to talk further about his expectations. What else he'd likely unearth in the trench. How he'd be presenting it. Funding possibilities...

Until, notwithstanding his genuine interest in the conversation, he'd allowed his gaze to wander to a second collapsible table erected a few hundred yards to the south of the trench. This one absent a sunshade. But nonetheless the center of a great deal of energetic activity.

First, three street children had dragged the table into position. Positioning it and securing its legs as Adrian and his friend had spoken. And then, having satisfied themselves as to the stability of the table, they'd concentrated with serious intensity on arranging a display of something heavy overtop of the cloth that covered it. Adrian hadn't quite been able to decipher the nature of their wares.

He had, though, noted that the children had been the same age and wearing much the same clothing as the girl who sold leaking pens and sandpaper-like facial tissue beneath the Consulate's founders sculpture when she wasn't being chased off by the two Marines assigned to that duty. And as such, they'd interested Adrian. Even as his

friend had spoken. One of the children—a boy—
had been wearing a t-shirt advertising the terrorist
boy band.

His friend, noting his interest, had grinned
even more broadly. Exposing gold-capped molars.
"You see? Sutton Hoo." He'd nodded in the
direction of the table. "They're already selling
fakes."

"Fakes?"

"Fakes. Forgeries. Knockoffs." His friend had
opened another bottle of water. "In preparation
for the tourists."

"But how do they know what to—to fake?"

"Those kids," his friend had said with
overlapping respect and despair, "are like the rats.
They're everywhere. You can't get rid of them.
We tip them not to steal anything. But we can't
prevent them from photographing it. Their pimps
give them disposable cameras." He was thoughtful
for a few seconds. "Some of them are real artists.
It's a shame."

Adrian had squinted across the dig toward the
objects on the table. From where he'd stood,
they'd looked no different from what his friend
had exposed in the trench. Cleaner, perhaps. But
otherwise, identical. Roundish humanoid statues,
the largest no bigger than a pint glass, most of them
the size of a misshapen tennis ball. All intricately
carved with expressive facial features, fingers, toes,
ornaments.

And then, feeling foolish he'd addressed his
friend. "Can I buy one?"

"Why not?"

"I mean," Adrian had fumbled for the words, "is it, you know, illegal?"

His friend had half-shrugged. Refusing to answer a stupid question. After which, finishing off his second bottle of water, he'd said, "if you want a good one, you ought to buy it now. The *Daily Republic* will be here tomorrow morning. They're running a front-page story on the dig. There will be motorcoaches full of Germans here by midweek." He'd slapped his chest again. "And I'll be Heinrich Schliemann!"

Adrian had already been fishing his wallet out of his pocket. Thanking his friend—and wishing him good luck with the Germans—he'd approached the table. After which, without negotiating, he'd bought twelve of the fake rock statues—six females and six males. Thinking, with an absurd romanticism that was very much unlike him, that they might want to consort with one another. Handing over to the children all of the cash he'd had on hand.

The children, thrilled by their good luck, had capered after his Fiat for a good quarter mile, waving his cash in the air, before giving up and returning to the dig and their table. And Adrian, cradling his plastic sack in his lap, had looked ahead to the *Oppenheimer* with more composure than he'd imagined possible. Casting his mind ahead to when he'd return the rocks to his rooms in the old part of the city. To examine and enjoy at his leisure.

19

NOW, however, he held the sack with one hand and extended his other hand toward Callie. After a moment of hesitation, looking as unenthusiastic to see Adrian as he was to see her, she took it. Jiggled it limply and let it go. Then, gesturing vaguely to the cockpit of the *Oppenheimer*, she indicated that they ought to board.

As he climbed up after her, she turned and eyed the sack. "What's that?"

Embarrassed, thinking she might be expecting a gift, Adrian held the sack closer to his side. "Rocks."

"Rocks?"

"Yes." He thought quickly, but not quickly enough. "I'm looking after them for a friend."

She settled herself onto one of the cushions in the cockpit—the air sufficiently warm that they'd remain above deck for the duration of the tour. Then, lowering her eyes, she picked at a ragged cuticle. Drawing blood.

"Oh."

Adrian, sitting across from her, folded his arms over his sack and waited, tense, as the boat left the dock, unwilling to lose anything overboard. Irrationally, he was beginning to associate the rocks in the sack with his personal well-being. Fearing for them as he might fear for himself or for his family.

His family in the abstract, that is. He'd never worried all that much about his mother or his father. They were the sort of people who could care for themselves. Unlike the rocks. He tightened his grip on the sack.

Neither he nor Callie spoke further.

Until, fifteen minutes later, once the boat had fought through its first colossal wake—thrown up by a menacing destroyer manned by sailors wearing the uniform of the empire to the north—a silent, deferential, and unsmiling member of the crew placed food in front of them. Something damp and purple, involving cephalopods. And as Callie picked at the stuff, she began to throw out desultory, abortive conversational gambits.

Adrian refused to help her along. Clutching his sack and limiting himself to bread rolls, he made no attempt to engage her. His goal was boorishness. To earn for himself the worst possible report—and ideally to tarnish Elaine in the process.

To his exasperation, however, his vacuous silences only seemed to encourage Callie. And as darkness fell, and as the *Oppenheimer*'s festive and unnecessary lights were illuminated, she began, diffidently, to open up to him. To make herself vulnerable. While he continued to clench the sack tightly enough that his fingernails bored into the palms of his hands, drawing his own blood. Wishing that it all would simply end.

"My father thinks I'm crazy," she was saying.
"Why?" Sullen.
"My son tried to kill me."
"Oh."

21

A non-sequitur, as far as Adrian could tell. But not one that he felt like exploring. Though the casual mention of a son did lead him silently to question the rumors of lesbianism.

"Do you know why he tried to kill me?" She appeared attached to the subject, despite Adrian's complete lack of interest.

"No." He bit back the obvious retort as too cruel. His goal was tedious, not sadistic. Besides, she might like sadistic.

"He said," she reflected dreamily, "that he mistook me for a bear."

"Were you dressed as a bear?"

"I don't think so."

He frowned. "You don't know? I mean, whether you were dressed as a bear or not?" This might explain her father's concerns about her mental equilibrium. Not, he insisted to himself, that he cared.

"It's difficult sometimes. To know. My son has—problems." She pushed aside the dish of purple tentacles. "This isn't very good."

"No," he agreed.

And then, he didn't know why—for he felt little regard or respect for Callie, and he'd never felt any need to confide in anyone before, and certainly not in a nebulous cipher like the thing wavering in and out of intelligibility across from him—he told her about his dream. His fantasy. The fantasy he'd harbored since childhood. The one about the flood.

Everyone wiped out. Everyone gone No conversation. No demands. Pure, beautiful nothingness. The feel of empty earth under his hands like the feel against his fingertips of the stone carvings he currently cradled in his lap. A complete absence of anything living.

Indeed, he talked at length. While she listened. And by the time he'd finished his recitation, the *Oppenheimer* was mooring, and she was smiling at him from the other side of the cockpit. Still vague. Distant. Though she did let him hand her down to the dock.

"My father expects us to go out again tomorrow evening," she said as they left the boat behind them.

Adrian stumbled to a horrified stop. His stomach dropping, reacting to his delayed realization of just how thoroughly he'd failed in his plan. He'd never rid himself of the obligation now. Of the lunatic Consul General's daughter.

Gripping the handles of the sack of rocks, he stared down at the ground and stalked forward once more. Unwilling to respond. Cursing the unfathomable desire to babble, to expose himself, that had possessed him on the boat. What could he possibly have been thinking?

"I'm sorry," she said, sounding as though she meant it. "It's only one more voyage. He'll let it go after that. It's a busy time of the year. Other crises to occupy him."

Adrian glanced over at her. Didn't speak.

23

"I hope you enjoy your rocks tonight," she offered.

"I told you," he said, churlish now, "they aren't mine. I'm looking after them for a friend."

"Your friend's rocks, then." She held out her hand. "Goodnight."

He took it, shook it as limply as she'd shaken his, and turned away, in search of his Fiat. The Consulate's black stretch Cadillac SUV was idling near the dockside, waiting for Callie.

ADRIAN found the next day that he couldn't bear to be parted from at least a selection of his stone statuettes. And so, as he left his rooms for the Consulate in the morning, he carried the smallest, a male, in his jacket pocket, while he brought three others—two females and a male—in his briefcase. Upon his arrival, he switched on the yellow light of his desk lamp and arranged the four rocks in each of the four corners of his square office. Pleased by the effect.

After that, he spoke to them. All day. Incessantly and steadily. Though it was only in the early afternoon that he recognized his interactions with them as, in fact, speech—and speech, moreover, that divulged, with great garrulity, secret thoughts and desires that he'd hardly ever admitted even to himself. Thoughts and desires that, under ordinary circumstances, were perhaps best not consigned to language.

Though surprised by this change in his ordinarily reticent personality, however, Adrian felt

24

little concern about it. His new vulnerability, if such it was, struck him as liberating rather than as damaging. His openness like an act of creation—the population of a new world, and a world all for himself. Something finally active in what had otherwise been his ferociously apathetic life.

Thus, when Elaine, still wearing the sunglasses, began to hover about his office later on in the afternoon, he merely laughed and welcomed her. She, too, showed no surprise at Adrian's shift away from cold, closed, and morose. Rather, lifting one of the stone statues—a pint-glass-sized male—she held it to the light, appraised it, and then settled it back into place.

"Nice piece," she commented.

"I like it."

"Local, isn't it?"

"But fake," he reassured her. "Entirely fabricated. Modern material."

"Of course." She touched her sunglasses and changed the subject. "By the way, Callie's father wants me to meet her tonight once the *Oppenheimer* has docked. A consular function the daughter's scheduled to attend." She smiled her empty smile. "I'm the chaperone."

"As long as it's not me." Joking. Jovial.

"Not yet." Failed jovial. And then, as she left the room: "you owe me a meeting."

STILL unable to separate himself from them—to imagine a scenario in which he couldn't touch them whenever the urge took him—Adrian

25

brought two of the statuettes (a male and a female) along with him to the dock, leaving two to guard his office. And when Callie began, in her bleary way, to converse with him after the boat cleared the oil tanker that nearly ran them down, he chose to facilitate rather than to block her advances. Trusting her word that her father would tire of whatever scheme he'd devised for them. Trusting, above all, the rocks.

Aside from which, Adrian was beginning to appreciate Callie. Speaking to her, he thought, was like speaking to the rocks. Calming. Empty. Not quite human. The conversations about which he'd fantasized for as long as he could remember. The conversations that he'd spent decades enjoying with himself, but that he'd never hoped to enjoy with another person. Outside of his head, that is.

When he went below to use the toilet, therefore, he was unprepared for Callie's betrayal of him. Or—as he'd gradually come to think of the two of them together—of *them*. And indeed, it was only when he heard the splash and the dismayed yell of the waiter, that he began to wonder whether Callie was less well-adjusted than he'd believed. Less enamored than he was of their unprecedented connection.

Moreover, by the time he'd disentangled himself from the pump toilet and made his way to the deck, the situation was beyond repair. For a brief second, he saw an anemic hand above the waves. And then a ripple. And then the hydrofoil airport shuttle sped over both of them, leaving nothing behind but a thin line of dirty foam.

Adrian's first reaction to the tragedy was surprised bewilderment. But then, centering himself—though he wasn't unduly de-centered by the, after all, comparatively small commotion in the water—he went into action. First, he calmed the waiter, who was kneeling against the boat's broken lifelines, making small wheezing noises. And second, in his broken approximation of the local language, he assured the skipper that he, Adrian, would take full responsibility for the accident. That no blame would fall on the crew.

And finally, third, once their story was established, Adrian returned, serene and focused, to the cockpit, where he extracted his stone statuettes from the canvas bag in which he'd transported them and arranged them on the cushions where Callie had once sat. Jaunty and social. Staring across the cockpit at him, enjoying their tour of the water.

As the *Oppenheimer* limped back to the dock, Adrian resumed with the rocks the conversation that he had broken off with Callie. Struck by the uninterrupted momentum of the exchange. Impressed, as he had been that afternoon, by the unparalleled empathy of the ancient stones. Certainly more than he'd elicited from Callie, even in her dreamier, more distant moods.

And thus, by the time the boat had moored, and he saw Elaine—still sporting the sunglasses—

27

strolling down the dock to receive them, Adrian felt more than confident about the situation. More than social. For the first time in his life, he felt love.

All of which meant that when Elaine reached the boat's ladder, he did nothing more than jump up from the cockpit cushions to wave at her. A touch frenetic. Giddy rather than melancholy or forlorn. The hydrofoil and its dirty streak of foam having slipped his mind—the pale hand sinking below the ripples expunged from his thoughts entirely.

She nodded back to him and boarded the boat. Then she examined the cockpit. Wrinkled her forehead.

"Where's Callie?"

"There." He indicated the female rock.

"Where?"

"Here." He lifted the rock and handed it to Elaine.

Elaine nodded slowly. Then she licked her lips, actually lifted the sunglasses, and cocked her head at the stone she was holding. After that, she let the sunglasses fall into place and secured the statuette under one arm. Smiled up at Adrian.

"Well, that solves a shitload of problems." She held out her other hand for Adrian to help her disembark. "The Consul General will be grateful."

When they reached the dock and began walking cordially in the direction of the car park, she continued. "You've done well, Adrian. Very well."

"It was a pleasure," he said, meaning it.

"And do see me in my office for that chat tomorrow, will you?"

He nodded. Pulled out the keys to his Fiat. Glanced over at her, thinking for the first time that the sunglasses were, after all, stylish. Though the skirt suit continued to remind him of espionage thrillers from the 1960s.

"Of course. I'm looking forward to it."

He positioned the male statuette in the passenger's seat such that it could see out the window. And then, all the way to his rooms in the old part of the city, making his way slowly through the evening traffic, he chatted with it. Communed with it. Opened himself up to it. Unaware of the passage of time. Unaware of anything but the haunting eyes of the rock. In love.

ARROWS

WHAT do you do with the gold ones?"
Elaine, wearing both her sunglasses and ear
protection, moved closer. Hoping to force an
error. She could feel the disgust radiating off of
him, and she liked the feeling.

But Rhys remained calm. Ignoring her, he
shot six holes into the paper target and then pulled
it toward them both. One hole. Not six. Perfect.
Though he'd have been surprised and
disappointed had it not been perfect.

He turned back to her and removed his ear
coverings. He hadn't heard her, but he'd read her
lips in the reflection off the plexiglass booth.
Besides, she never varied her tired interrogation
tactics. Persistence, he imagined, rather than
intelligence was the explanation for her successes.

Not that he paid attention to her tactics or, for
that matter, her successes. Rhys commanded the
Marine contingent responsible for the Consul
General's safety. Elaine was an "Economic Affairs
Liaison." They had little to say to one another. He
wished she'd leave him in peace.

She scooped up the small cardboard container of ammunition he'd left beside him on a shelf as he secured his weapon. Reminiscent of a mid-century carton of cigarettes. Decorated by the sort of women who used to adorn fighter jets. The rosy and peachy body parts glinted off the lenses of her sunglasses and then blurred as she held it up closer to her face to examine it.

After a few seconds, she rattled it playfully and grinned at him, knowing perfectly well what it contained, even without peeking inside. His specials. The gold ones.

"What do you do with the gold ones?" she repeated.

"None of your business, ma'am." He extended his hand. After a brief pause, she returned it to him. Choosing her battles.

He secured the box in a pocket of his shirt. Smoothing down his uniform. Then he walked, stolid, away from the range and up the concrete steps leading to the food court. She pushed her hands into her pockets and followed.

Nor did she cease to follow him when he reached the crowded cafeteria. And neither did she desist from purchasing the same bottle of water and the same blueberry muffin from the same counter, or sitting across from him at the same unstable wire and plastic table. Observing the gallery and the LED sconces. Calculated and infuriating.

When he merely continued to stare into the middle distance, eating his muffin, she spoke again. "Do you mind if I join you?"

They'd been sitting in silence for close to two minutes. Both had nearly finished their food. "No, ma'am."

She opened her water and took a small sip. "Really, Rhys. Why do you bother?"

"Bother with what, ma'am?"

"This." Gesturing about the atrium. "All of it?"

"My duty, ma'am."

She laughed. "You're ornamental, Rhys. A decoration. You've got no duty here."

Since she hadn't asked a question, he didn't reply. His face impassive, he placed his paper napkin over the remains of his muffin. His other hand, Elaine noted, was clenched into a fist in his lap.

"Your uniformed boys are a retinue, Rhys. Props. Prancing about as eye candy to entertain the masses as the Consul does *his* duty." She took another swig of her water. "If anyone is responsible for security here, it's I. I target. I eliminate." She paused. "You adorn yourself with fancy looking bullets."

"Thank you, ma'am." He stood and collected the detritus of his muffin. "Good afternoon."

She watched him leave, pleased by her progress. And when he unconsciously clutched the container of golden ammunition in his pocket as he left the food court, she smiled. She still had no idea how or where he used it. But she'd gotten to him. Then she leaned back in her chair and finished her water.

Fucking Marines. A military coup waiting to happen. A significant portion of her time at the Consulate was spent seeing to it that the Marine contingent remained confused and off-balance. Starting with Rhys and ending with the healthy childlike recruits he commanded—many of whom, despite their physical presence in the Republic, couldn't locate the country, or likely the continent from which it dangled, on a map. Frolicking about like nymphs on an island untethered to any seabed.

WHEN Elaine reached her office on the fourth floor of the Consulate, she closed and carefully locked her door before allowing the smile to fade from her features. Then she pulled the blind over her large window—the view of the suburb, with its angry, unburied ghosts and its fencing wire did little for her—lowered herself into her cushioned desk chair, and removed her sunglasses. Cracked her knuckles. Rubbed her reddened eyes, the glasses hooked over the joint of one finger.

After a moment or two of silent misery, she balanced the sunglasses on top of Callie, the rock's, head. Raised her hand in a weak greeting to it. A permanent addition to her office now—the Consul General more than relieved to have the girl off his hands—the rock pleased Elaine with its air of solid, ancient wisdom. The purity of its desire—a desire so far removed from the unspeakable, twisted thing that was her own that it might have been the product of an entirely alien brain chemistry. On occasion, she even caught herself speaking to it.

At the moment, however, preferring not to be observed, she turned the thing away. Considered the snaky hair carved into the back of its head, grateful that it wasn't currently judging her. And then, opening the bottom drawer of her desk, she retrieved a three-quarters-full bottle of vodka.

Holding it in one hand, she paused for a moment over the smaller bottle of fermented goat's milk that she sometimes used as a mixer. Concluding, however, that she needed straight potatoes today, she left the goat's milk in place and used her foot to push the drawer shut. Then she unscrewed the lid and, not troubling to locate a glass, swallowed three or four shots directly from the receptacle.

Her eyes closed, she waited a few seconds for the sting to hit her stomach. Followed by the warmth. Before, taking a smaller swallow, she re-capped the bottle and allowed herself to look at her desk calendar.

Seven years, two months, and three days. Close to two years left of her penance here. Quickly, she opened the drawer and replaced the bottle. Not in the mood to wake up on her office floor tomorrow morning. Though such mornings were by no means unfamiliar, she had work to do yet this evening. As well as tomorrow. Semi-conscious intoxication would not help with that.

Seven years, two months, and three days. Of a nine-year sentence passed on her for a single error. And an error of ethics, even, rather than of analysis or judgment. One bitch snake ruining her after a lifetime of success. She felt the alcohol spreading through her bloodstream, entering her brain.

No. Not a bitch snake, she corrected herself. A little wobbly now. Or, that is, not a bitch. Elaine herself was a bitch. A wolf-bitch, she liked to think. But the girl had been a snake, a serpent, something unmentionable...

She considered opening the drawer again, but then she forced herself to exert self-control. To remember her past with a modicum of sobriety. The years before her near-decade of forced labor in this cartoonish diplomatic backwater. Tormenting herself properly before beginning her nightly work.

Years ago—centuries, millennia, eternities, it felt—Elaine had been a philosopher. Her specialty, Wittgenstein. A risky choice as a mid-century graduate student equipped with her particular chromosomal combination, but Elaine had never been a coward. And she'd known, even at the age of twenty-two, that she, more than any of her male counterparts, possessed the talent for hair-splitting logic and near-suicidal self-loathing that was necessary to doing the master justice. She was his

proper heir. Not them. And she'd worked at it. And then, she'd succeeded.

In large part, it's true, her successes had been as much the product of her languages as they had her logic and her loathing. More often than not accidental—sitting bolt upright in bed at three in the morning with the sudden, chill realization that she could comprehend Serbo-Croatian—her language acquisition had been uncanny. Indeed, it still was. Still blindsiding her when she least expected it. Though she found it more an annoyance at this point than an advantage. Like a persistent skin lesion that changed shape sufficiently to cause concern, but insufficiently to merit a visit to the physician. As much as possible, she tried to ignore it.

At the age of twenty-two, however, she'd reveled in it. Well, in it and in the attention it had brought her. Because she could feel them— Them—watching from the moment her skills had hit the market. As a matter of course, she'd led them on. She herself scarcely out of childhood. Flirting through the back streets of Vienna—this in the years when Austria was still a noirish borderland of people in trench coats with no fixed abode rather than the likely future setting of the terrorist boy band's great Eurovision triumph. Dropping the metaphorical handkerchief in their path. A billet-doux or two.

But they hadn't approached her then. They hadn't even made their interest definitive. On the contrary, even as she'd beckoned to them, showing them coyly what she'd got, they'd waited—patient and composed—for seven long years before initiating contact. Seven years as she'd finished her graduate work, taken her exalted university position, published her groundbreaking monograph, and then secured tenure. So that after the period of breathless waiting, the contact, when it finally had come, had been a bit of an anticlimax. In fact, if she was honest with herself—which Elaine always was—it had been a categorical disappointment.

The diffident, self-effacing man who'd finally insinuated himself into her walnut office with its mullioned windows that autumn afternoon two decades ago had been as far removed from her Mephistophelian fantasies as an individual possibly could be. He'd tripped over her wastepaper basket. For the first two minutes, she'd believed he'd come to purchase old textbooks from her.

Moreover, the request that he'd made of her had been laughable. Close to insulting. Placing his grubby business card on her desk, he'd asked her to pass along the names of students looking to expand their extracurricular activities. Any, that is, with unusual skills, similar to her own, that might prove marketable beyond academia.

She'd used one finger to pull the frayed card closer to her. Feeling more like a procurer than—well, whatever it was that she'd always thought she'd be. But they—They—had reached a decision as to how she might best serve them. And there was, it seemed, as the little man had bowed his way out of her office, little that she could do to alter their opinion of her. She'd been recruited.

As always, they'd been correct. Their appraisal of her talents had been as frighteningly accurate as it had been demeaning. And as years—and then more than a decade—had passed, Elaine had funneled to them an unending supply of pristine minds to field. Minds to consume and to discard. Minds in the service of their mission.

Within a few months of embarking on her unofficial work for them, in fact, she'd already developed the strategy of seduction that rivaled in effectiveness those of the most ruthless of her competitors. The strategy that cemented her reputation. The strategy that, within the narrow confines her cohort, made her famous. Untouchable.

Identifying the target was easy. A week or two into a seminar, it became obvious which potential recruits were vulnerable and which were not. Meaning that by the third or fourth week, Elaine was able to ignore the latter while focusing on, and encouraging, the former—gradually reassuring herself that her chosen marks were: a) intelligent enough to realize that they weren't the best and never would be (the stupid ones never got it); b) arrogant enough to be bothered by this realization (the confident ones didn't care); and c) brittle enough to hate themselves for both their failure and for their neurosis. People, in other words, like Elaine herself.

Once she'd reassured herself as to their
vulnerability, she'd had little to do but wait for the
weakness to manifest itself. Inevitably, there would
come the moment of humiliation. The moment
when, arrogant, her targets overreached themselves
in a public discussion, and then, brittle, were
shattered by their error.

At which point, still smarting, they would be
invited into Elaine's office. Offered tea. Persuaded,
in the gentlest of possible ways, that the reason for
the humiliation had not been their own, varied,
Achilles' heels, but rather the envy of their peers.
And who wouldn't be envious? Such intelligence.
Such rigorous, yet creative, analysis. And, across
the desk, they were already rolling over for her.

She'd had so many by her second decade of
teaching that she couldn't even remember their
names. Or, for that matter, what had become of
them once she'd diddled them and sent them on
their way. True, a few of the discarded husks
contacted her months or years after their
flameouts, blaming her for their unhappiness. But
that was what spam folders were for. And a few
even balked at joining the team in the first place,
once their time had arrived. The one who had
tricked her—asking for a last favor and then
requesting, as that favor, his release from the
contract—had been her favorite. Cheeky boy. He
was teaching at some liberal arts college now. Still
chaste.

Or, more notorious, the brilliant, troublesome
one who'd simply refused to comply altogether

after she'd made the promise. Elaine, in a rage, had driven that one mad. Setting her up at the pinnacle of the intellectual world and then seeing to it that no one, ever, trusted her work. Not a book. Not an article. Not a review. No grants, no fellowships, no paltry little stipends. The girl got nothing. And so, isolated and marooned in her greatness, she'd slowly disintegrated. Elaine, of course, could have done worse to her, but she'd been pleased by the intricacy of the retaliation she'd organized. And so, she'd let it alone.

All of which meant that her career with them—Them—had in general fared better than any individual working for them across twenty years had the right to expect. That is, until the arrival of the bitch snake. Snake. Not bitch. A touch dizzy, despite having returned the bottle to the drawer, Elaine massaged her forehead with her fingertips.

She'd known from the beginning that the snake was a faulty target. Confident rather than arrogant. And not even all that intelligent. Worst of all, though—unlike the others—the snake had known that Elaine was seducing her. She'd played along with the process as a kind of game. And her capitulation had felt theatrical. Not quite genuine. Which, as it transpired, had in fact been the case.

When, a few months after the snake had been launched into the field, the diffident little man had appeared at Elaine's door—for the first time in fifteen years, and looking not a day older—Elaine had guessed that he'd been coming about the snake. And indeed, looking pained, he'd pushed a badly bound novel across the desktop at her. Watching her reaction.

Elaine hadn't touched it. "What's that?"

"She's written a book," he'd replied mournfully.

"As a whistleblower? Haven't you protocols in place to deal with that sort of thing?"

"No," he'd intoned. "A novel."

"So?"

"About Republican Rome."

"I don't understand."

"It's an allegory."

"Oh, for God's sake." She'd pushed the book back at him. "Who cares?"

"She's turning our people." He'd rubbed his temples with his fingertips. "Our lines of communication are fraying. We've lost contact with the center."

"So, what am I supposed to do about it?" Elaine had abruptly stood. The man's stillness had bothered her. "I don't do fieldwork. Thanks to you."

The man had frowned, retrieved the book, secured it carefully in his briefcase, and shambled from the room. Two days later, Elaine had purchased a ticket to Vienna—still, if anemically, a Wittgenstein specialist—where she'd tracked down the snake and killed her. A carving knife through the navel. Effective if not pretty. The best she could do, not having been trained for anything beyond talent spotting.

41

She'd believed the problem solved, and had returned to her teaching still irritated, but by no means concerned. Vowing to take a holiday from them—Them—sometime very soon. When the little man had appeared in her office yet again, however, she'd known that her confidence had been misplaced. She'd almost been expecting it.

Looking even more bilious than he had before, he'd settled himself into the same chair. And then, without speaking, he'd pushed toward her a manila envelope containing tickets, instructions, and an itinerary. After which, he'd stood, still silent, and left the room.

She'd known what was inside even without opening it. But she hadn't known the extent of it. And when she'd forced herself to examine the papers—later, after purchasing the first in a long series of increasingly ineffective bottles of vodka—she'd thrown up what she'd compelled herself to drink. Nine years. Nine years they'd given her. Nine years as a slave to the nonentity that was the Consul General.

And, of course, his batty daughter. Deciding that she didn't mind Callie watching after all, Elaine turned the rock back around. Patted it familiarly on the head. The University, upon learning of the tragic and inexplicable death of the snake in Vienna had endowed a scholarship in her name. Something to do with athletics, Elaine believed, but she'd tried not to pay attention. It only made her angry.

And now, here she was, seven years, two months, and three days later, still toiling. Doing her best to bring the place down around her ears. Even as she did her duty. Much like Rhys was doing his duty. Rhys. A promising target. Upstanding. Vindictive. It would be interesting to see how he responded to her goading. She predicted something subtle.

THE bullet that streaked past her, grazed her lower leg, and embedded itself in the base of the founders sculpture was a stray. Accidental. But even before she saw the glint of the gold, she knew that Rhys had sent it to her. As a warning.

Entertained, she squatted and used a penknife to dig it out of the concrete. Ignoring the run in her stocking and the trickle of blood that was pooling below her ankle. One of his own Marines had apparently been injured in much the same way earlier today. One hoped that he—Rhys—wasn't becoming sloppy.

Pocketing the golden bullet, she straightened, stretched her back, and noticed the street girl peering at her from behind Our Great Founder's booted foot. Her eyes glazed. Scratchy breathing from the glue she'd inhaled and stuffed back into a grubby pocket moments before Elaine's arrival.

The girl was wearing a sort of smock tied with a braided cord of ivy. Barefoot. No wares to sell today—or perhaps she'd already rid herself of whatever her pimp had imposed on her that morning. Either way, Elaine ignored her. Unlike the entry-level officers, Elaine never engaged in commerce with the girl.

The girl, however, frequently put herself in the way of Elaine. Which was odd given that she ordinarily ran from the higher echelons of the Consular staff—possessed of a telepathic sense of who was likely to purchase pens, toothbrushes, facial tissue, boxes of "Channel #5" perfume, or whatever her pimp had procured for redistribution, and who was likely to have her carted away somewhere unthinkable. Elaine, intuitively, ought to have belonged to the latter category in the girl's world.

And yet, the girl always stood her ground. Gazing at Elaine. The only person attached to the Consulate, in fact, including the Consul General himself, who wasn't at least a touch disconcerted by the flashing lenses of her sunglasses.

If Elaine was troubled by the girl's interest (she was), she didn't let on. Instead, with a brief nod, straightening the sunglasses, she turned on her heel and made her way back into the fortress. Going in search of Rhys. Pleased by the physical as well as metaphorical ammunition he'd provided her that morning. Things were heating up. And the small pain where the bullet had abraded the skin of her leg only made her smile.

Rhys was in the basement, shooting. Again. When he saw her reflection in the plexiglass, however, he stopped what he was doing, removed his ear protection, and secured his weapon.

Turned in her direction. Almost as though he'd been expecting her and hoping for her arrival. His impassive face came close to hinting at happiness.

Elaine, perturbed by his apparent pleasure, slowed, fingered the golden bullet in her pocket, and went on the offensive. "I understand you've all had an exciting day, Rhys."

"Ma'am?"

"Two rounds of ammunition wildly off course. One severe injury. One close call."

He clasped his hands behind his back. "Yes, ma'am. I take full responsibility."

"Do you?"

He nodded. "Yes, ma'am. A miscalculation. Faulty aim."

"You don't miscalculate, Rhys."

"Thank you, ma'am."

She narrowed her eyes. He was, unquestionably, happy. The skin to the side of his mouth was twitching faintly. She'd never seen the movement before, and she didn't like it.

"I've been asked to investigate," she informed him, still aggressive.

"Yes, ma'am."

"I'll be speaking to your wounded Marine."

"Yes, ma'am." The twitching around his mouth was now pronounced.

"He's on site, correct? At the clinic?"

"Yes, ma'am."

"Is there information you'd like to pass on to me before I begin?" she persisted, becoming almost alarmed by his relaxed reaction to the conversation.

Sensing her disquiet, he controlled his smile. His face blank once more. "No, ma'am. I have full confidence that Private Laurence will demonstrate compliance."

"Good." She examined his expressionless features. "I'd hate to see you blamed for this."

"Ma'am."

Dissatisfied by the outcome of her conversation, but curious—her fatal flaw—about the state of the injured Marine, Elaine set off for the Consulate's clinic on the fifth floor of the building. Though the Republic's healthcare was globally recognized for its excellent (if heavy-handed and historically mildly genocidal) qualities—far better than what got served up as medicine in their own country—Consular officials were nonetheless required to take their medical concerns to a collection of imported native physicians lodged in an annex on the upper two floors of the fortress. To be healed by fellow citizens who carried the proper passports. In-house.

It was a particularly strange situation, Elaine had always felt, in that a good sixty percent of the diplomatic incidents that the Consul General found himself smoothing over had to do with medical tourists from his own country dissatisfied by the facelifts and aesthetic dentistry they'd purchased in the Republic. Here, especially, it made little sense to confine medical practice to political, or, in the case of the Consulate, to extraterritorial, borders. And not for the first time, Elaine found herself wishing that her compatriots would limit their national pride to voyages on the *Oppenheimer*.

But then, dismissing the thought, she pushed through to Private Laurence's recovery room. At least the clinic was convenient. And though she'd once concerned herself with healing—curiosity again—the profession really was better off rationalized and overseen by experts. Not her domain.

They'd housed him in one of the nicer units. A window to the outside. Natural sunlight. No additional beds in the room. Flowers already arranged in vases, and a selection of graphic novels, heavy on the superheroes, stacked on a table to his side. A small tray next to the flowers held the cleaned bullet. A souvenir. Laurence's first action.

Elaine crossed the room to examine the bullet. It was a dullish leaden color. Not one of Rhys's specials, then. She placed it with a clatter back into the tray.

The sound brought Laurence out of his shallow sleep, and he looked about the room with confusion. Charming confusion. No more than twenty-one or twenty-two years old, his military haircut beginning to grow long, and his covers pulled up over his chest, he reminded Elaine of a boy unwillingly dragged out of bed for school. Wanting nothing more than to sneak back under the blankets with a light and one of the comic books.

Or—she peered at him more carefully—not a boy. Not at all, in fact. She was observing him with some intensity now. On the contrary, there was something else in his eyes, since he'd opened them, that set him apart from the other Marines. Something she could see quite clearly, but that she hadn't expected. Laurence was intelligent. Logical. And, above all, vulnerable.

She made a sound that might have been taken by those who didn't know her as a gasp. He was like her, she gradually realized. He belonged to her. He simply didn't understand it yet. Her pulse began to race.

So astonished was she by what she'd drawn from Private Laurence's eyes, that she failed for three or four seconds to register the hatred with which he in turn regarded her. But when she did see it, she paid it little attention. They all hated her. That was nothing new. And Laurence, she was confident, would learn quickly to stifle it.

A uniquely brilliant boy, she thought to herself. Shining. All she had to do was lead him with stern conviction toward the proper decision, such that he never quite grasped that an alternative choice had been possible. And if anyone knew how to accomplish that feat, Elaine did.

Thus, like returning to a half-forgotten athletic skill, she began.

"Good afternoon, Private Laurence. I'm here to complete a report on the incident this morning. You may call me Elaine." She flourished a pen and a clipboard that she had no intention of using.

"Yes, ma'am," he muttered. No eye contact.

"First, I must examine the wound. I'll call a nurse if you'd prefer—"

"No, ma'am," he interrupted, flipping over on his stomach and pulling the blanket down with one hand. "Unnecessary."

She smiled to herself. Textbook. He'd try to embarrass her. Twenty-two-year-old boys were unfamiliar with elderly women incapable of embarrassment. He likely thought of her as a sort of spinster aunt.

"Thank you." She approached the bed and pulled the blanket down further. Her smile became wry. Rhys had shot the boy cleanly through the right buttock. The wound couldn't have been more recognizably the Commander's work had he signed it. The question, still, was why.

More important than why Rhys had targeted the Private, however, was how to alter the Private's attitude toward herself. As she gazed down at the boy's injury, her earlier impressions of his intelligence and potential swelled into something close to overwhelming. She needed him. It had been years since she'd encountered a likelier quarry.

Nonetheless, she continued to work slowly. Carefully. Avoiding the slightest possibility of a misstep. Tilting her head, she prodded the area around the wound with her fingertip. Enjoying the stiffening of his body as she did so. The small grunt muffled in the pillow. His refusal to admit to pain.

"Thank you, Private." She stepped back. "You may face me."

He flipped onto his back, winced again, unused to his body failing him, and glared venomously across at her. "Yes, ma'am."

"Would you like to tell me what happened?"

"No, ma'am."

She nodded. "Let me phrase that in a different way. What happened?"

"I can't remember, ma'am."

"Nothing at all?"

"Nothing, ma'am."

"Ah." She made a meaningless mark on the clipboard. Then she set it beside the graphic novels on the table. "Your loyalty does you credit, Private. I wonder, were you aware that my own Staff Sergeant was recently promoted to a position at the Embassy?"

"No, ma'am."

"We could use a man like you," she said, "as a military attaché. Loyal. Intelligent." She allowed herself to smile. "Impervious to pain."

"Thank you, ma'am."

"Consider it," she told him, gathering up her clipboard, resettling her sunglasses, and turning toward the door.

"Yes, ma'am." His tone made it clear that he found the offer reprehensible.

Once again, Elaine didn't mind. They always came around in the end. Watching the conversion was part of the pleasure.

But, as it turned out, Laurence didn't come around. If anything, he became surlier and less tractable the more he saw her. Visibly offended by her presence whenever she visited. And she did visit frequently. Every morning. Sometimes in the afternoons as well. She couldn't help it. Ignoring Rhys entirely now, whose obvious and flagrant grin was beginning to annoy her. She wondered whether he might be sampling the street girl's glue. Something to check on when she'd sorted the Private Laurence situation.

When a week had passed, and Laurence was still immovable, however, she determined that she'd need a new strategy. More pressure. Thus far, he hadn't budged.

Nodding at him and setting her clipboard on the table, she once again approached the bed. Pushed her hand into one pocket and fingered the golden bullet she still carried about with her, though she didn't quite know why.

"I must re-examine the wound," she said. "I'll call a nurse—"

"No, ma'am." He turned onto his stomach and pulled down the blankets. "Unnecessary."

It was almost as though he believed that a nurse witnessing her observation of him would be dishonorable. Shameful. Surprising herself, Elaine

51

began to feel offended. And she couldn't remember the last time another person had managed to offend her.

When she saw the entry wound, however, the new and uncomfortable emotion dissipated, and she knitted her brows instead. The injury wasn't healing properly. In fact, it looked morbidly infected. Diseased. Wrong. At the very least, worrisome.

The skin was coarse and thickened, flaking off in strips, like bark, from the area surrounding the bullet hole. But it wasn't just his buttock that had been affected. Even from a small distance, Elaine could see that the infection was spreading out in all directions, up his lower back, over his right thigh, across his stomach, no doubt, should he turn over. She couldn't understand how neither the surgeons nor Laurence himself had commented on it. Or even Rhys.

Most troubling, though, was that when she pushed at the skin surrounding the wound, as she had before, Laurence didn't flinch. He didn't appear to feel it at all. Prone on his stomach. Bored, if anything. No grunt from the pillow.

"Do you feel this?" she finally asked.

"Feel what, ma'am?"

"Nothing." She spread her fingers over the infection that had moved across the back of his thigh. The skin was tough and jagged. Startled, she drew back her hand when something like a splinter lodged itself in her palm. She picked it out with the

52

thumb and index finger of her other hand. Squinting through the dark lenses of her glasses.

"Thank you," she said. "That will be all."

"Yes, ma'am."

He flipped back over. No reaction to landing on the wound. Though his voice, she thought, was deeper. Scratchier. Almost like the voice of the street girl under the founders sculpture. Perhaps they'd all been sampling her wares.

Regardless of the source of the change, Elaine was troubled. If the infection had reached his throat, it was surely a serious problem. And she didn't want to lose him before she'd converted him. He belonged to her, even if he didn't know it yet.

She moved to the foot of his bed, unhooked the physician's report, and perused it. No mention of an infection. No abnormality in the skin surrounding the wound. According to the medical staff, Laurence was healing typically.

She re-hooked the report and retrieved her clipboard. "Thank you, Private Laurence."

"Ma'am."

THIS was Rhys's doing. She didn't know how, but something about the scenario stank of him. And, of course, he'd been the one to shoot the poor child in the first place. For the first time in months, Elaine felt more angry than entertained by her ongoing, low grade war against the Marines. Not to mention almost—if not actually—frightened.

She found him, as usual, in the plexiglass booth in the basement. But he wasn't shooting. Instead, he was waiting for her. The same tiny smile moving the corners of his mouth. Definitely hitting the glue, she decided.

"There's something wrong with Private Laurence," she told him without preamble. "What are you going to do about it?"

"I don't understand, ma'am." His hands behind his back again.

"He's got an infection. It's spreading."

"The clinic hasn't informed me of any infection, ma'am." Lackadaisical.

"It was on the bullet," she fumed. "What did you put on the bullet?"

"Ma'am?"

"The skin," she informed him, "around his wound is turning stiff. Wrong. Not like skin at all. And his voice—"

"Is Private Laurence himself bothered by what you've seen? Pained?" He hadn't changed his position.

Elaine stared at him. Never in the seven years that she'd interacted with him had Rhys ever interrupted her. Never had he deigned to ask her a question. Something was very wrong. Also, he was still smiling. She removed her sunglasses and fixed him with a fully realized glare. It made no difference to his composure. Irritated, she replaced the glasses.

"Private Laurence," he continued, "has made his decision." The smile had left his face and

54

the more familiar cold hatred had replaced it. "Or you made it for him." He paused. "Ma'am."

She watched him standing straight and silent beside the plexiglass booth. And then, without speaking, she turned and strode up the concrete steps to the food court. Trotted up to the gallery. Reached the third floor, nodding to Adrian gossiping with his rocks in his new office. Began running at the fourth floor, and was panting, short of breath, by the time she pushed her way into Private Laurence's room.

The boy was in a sorry state. The infection had spread over both of his legs and his chest, sending tendrils up to his chin and his cheeks, stiffening his fingers. The blanket had fallen to the floor, and Elaine could see that the flaking layers of skin had broken through his hospital gown. Laurence was effectively naked, though he looked armored instead. Bits of sickening green were peeking out of the spaces between his toes and underneath his ears.

He was still breathing, but the respiration was labored. And his eyes were covered by greenish cataracts. He reacted not at all to Elaine's presence in the room. But then, he'd scarcely reacted when the roughened monstrosity that had colonized his body had been confined to his right buttock. She came close to weeping when she saw him.

After that, however, angry instead, she strode over to the bed and shook him by the shoulders. Tried to shake him. His body was so dense and heavy—as though the toughened matter that had overspread his skin had likewise pooled in his bones and veins—that she couldn't move him more than a few inches to the side. Giving up, she slapped his face. Which did nothing to his face, but did hurt her hand quite a lot.

Then, stepping back, she spoke to him. "Your choice? That's what Rhys said. *This?* Rather than me?"

A sound that almost wasn't a sound—a sort of sighing vibration, like a wind passing through a forest of conifers—travelled from his chest to his throat. It sounded to Elaine like laughter. Freedom. The sound the bitch snake had made before Elaine had shoved the carving knife into her navel.

"Oh, fuck you." She turned and left the room.

The next morning, however, repenting of her anger—still feeling the irritating pointed hook in her psyche that had pulled her back to his bedside over and over and over again throughout the previous weeks—she climbed the stairs to the fifth floor. Slowly this time. Clutching the golden bullet in her pocket. Uncertain that she wanted to see what had become of the boy.

When she reached his room, however, nothing was there. Though the agonizing hook in her soul was still very much embedded, Laurence himself was gone. The bed stripped of its blankets. The mattress bare. The graphic novels and the physician's chart removed. The window open, airing the room, despite the security risk.

She let her eyes wander the anonymous space. Refusing once again to let herself cry. At her age, tears were an abomination. And then, bemused, she noticed the table. The vases of flowers had been removed, but in their place was a small potted Ficus. Flourishing in the sunlight and air that flooded through the open window. A good tree for an office.

Elaine approached the tree and rubbed a few of its leaves between her thumb and index finger. She'd never been good at houseplants. But this one spoke to her. Shrugging, she lifted it and took it from the room. Returned to her own office. Placed it on a shelf under a window, just beside Callie, the rock. She'd also need to find herself a watering can. Then she removed her sunglasses and balanced them on top of Callie's stone head.

When she stepped back to examine the effect, she chided herself. Her intention upon arriving in this hellhole had been to leave the insulting office bare and impersonal. And yet now, over the past few weeks, she'd accumulated not only a piece of art, but a plant. A regular collection. All that were missing were family photos and a colorful plastic troll. A poster, perhaps, of a cat looking pained beneath an uplifting slogan.

Sighing, she lowered herself into her chair, opened the bottom drawer of her desk, and retrieved the bottle of vodka. Seven years, two months, and five days. She'd be drinking it straight again.

GRAPES

ON Tuesday, he gave her a pocketful of loose coins in exchange for a package of facial tissue that left him with a bumpy rash across his upper lip. On Wednesday, he gave her a bill in the lowest denomination printed by the Republic for a pair of toothbrushes that cut his gums into bloody ribbons. The bill was worth less than the spare change. On Thursday, she sold him the glue—

"Wait." Dolores finished the note she'd begun on the yellow pad. Folded her hands in her lap. "She sold you the glue?"

"No." Contrite. "Sorry. She gave it to me for nothing. A gift."

"Good. Thank you." She lifted her pen. "Go on."

But he'd lost his momentum. Befuddled and quiet, he looked to Dolores for guidance. His eyes bloodshot. His voice, when he'd been speaking, raspy.

She waited for a few seconds, encouraging. Nonjudgmental. But it was clear that he was fading. His red eyes began to glaze.

Before she lost him, she spoke. "We're talking today because you've been ill, Cecil. Do you remember? The transport truck? The girl?" She kept her calm eyes on his. "The glue?"

"No." He slumped in the chair. And then, before Dolores could prop him upright, he lost consciousness and slipped to the floor. With a muffled thump.

Dolores sighed and set her pad on a small table to the side of her own armchair. Cecil, one of two Marines assigned to remove the street children from their—the children's—base of operations at the edge of the Consulate's founders sculpture, had been brought to her two weeks ago under unprecedented circumstances. The details of those circumstances were unclear—not least because both Marines remained conscious for only minutes at a time, regardless of the various pharmaceutical cocktails that had been pumped into them since they'd been recovered. But from what Dolores had pieced together, the two had not only failed to rid the sculpture of the street children, but had absconded with one, a girl, in a stolen troop transport vehicle full of their—the Marines'—fellow Privates. Before embarking on a disorderly and highly public joyride throughout the city.

They'd been apprehended only when the truck had slammed through the ivy-covered wrought-iron fences that separated the road from one of the city's more exclusive waterfront dance clubs. Celebrities had been present. The Consul General had been forced to issue an apology.

Gratuities had changed hands. And the Ambassador himself, leaving a meeting concerning rare-earth metal extraction on the empty, frigid plateau, had openly reprimanded the Consular staff.

The only reason that Cecil and his counterpart were speaking with Dolores now rather than on their way to a court-martial was the unusual (unprecedented) state in which they'd been recovered. Both were intoxicated to the point of oblivion on glue, though neither had a history of substance abuse. Cecil himself hadn't even touched caffeine or alcohol—at least that witnesses had ever seen.

The girl—no more than eleven or twelve years old—had apparently been driving the vehicle. Or, that is, she'd been found in the driver's seat, calmly clutching the wheel. And the other Marines—nine, ten, perhaps as many as fifteen, according to the several reports collected throughout the city—were absent. Missing. Investigators couldn't even find bodies or body parts to assemble for the families.

As for the Consul General, he was not only declining to make a statement beyond his initial apology to the state-run news agencies, but he was declining to contact said families until he had a narrative that didn't involve glue and a street child. He didn't care what that narrative was. But volatile solvents and impudent waifs couldn't be a part of it. He'd locked himself in his office, refusing to emerge until someone emailed him a script.

Thus, Cecil was now lying on the floor of Dolores's consulting room. Gently snoring. His counterpart was sleeping in the clinic. And the girl, from what Dolores had heard, spent much of her time these days with Rhys. Who apparently got on with her.

Dolores lowered herself to her knees beside Cecil and patted his cheek. No response. Then she sat back on her heels, trying to decide whether to have him revived again for another few minutes.

Although ordinarily a gentle and understanding person, Dolores had become frustrated by this set of cases. She hadn't been trained for it. And she didn't want to land her charges in more trouble than they already faced. That is, when they finally woke up.

She worried less about herself. Grandfathered into her position at the Consulate, she was well insulated from both bureaucratic attack and retaliatory demotion or reassignment. Little could touch her. Little ever ruffled her.

Literally grandfathered into her position. She continued to peer down at Cecil's placid, tranquil face. Dolores's grandfather had been one of the first chaplains assigned to the Consulate when Our Great Founder had been in the process of hammering out the still-contested borders of the Republic—beginning his work, even, in the belle-époque building in the louche, "foreign" neighborhood during the troubled ("exciting") years that saw it transition from Ambassadorial to

Consular duties. He'd witnessed the initiating, and now celebrated, BDSM clubs coming into being. He'd watched the drug culture blossoming.

And so, a few years into his posting, he'd found himself understandably incapable of leaving the place. Adopting the city and the Republic as his own, her grandfather had married a scion of one of the few aristocratic families that had evaded the attentions of Our Great Founder, and had received permission from his connections back home to turn his temporary position into a lifelong career. Their daughter, Dolores's mother, had married a cousin of Our Great Founder, thereby erasing any residual monarchical stain. And Dolores, inheriting the Consular position from her grandfather when he'd become too old to perform it effectively—as "Mental Health Officer" rather than as "Chaplain," however—was thus among the Consulate's most influential figures in both the Republic she served and the Republic she represented. Or vice versa. Even the Consul General found her networks intimidating.

Not that Dolores flaunted her family. Like her grandfather and her mother—if, perhaps, less her father (Our Great Founder's relatives were a colorful lot)—she was a humble person. A great believer in hard work and responsibility. And, of course, sobriety.

She tightened her lips, looking down at Cecil, who continued to snore on her floor. She'd picked up hints over the past months that the glue was becoming a problem among the newer Marine recruits. But she'd had no idea that the taint was so deeply entrenched. So infectious.

Without hesitation, Dolores blamed the street children and their pimps for the contagion. In fact, if anyone had asked her—though she was glad that no one did—she'd have told them outright that she believed the children not to be properly Republican at all. Agents provocateurs sent by the empire to the north. Out to weaken Republican constitutions. Both types of constitution.

But no one did ask. And she kept her beliefs quiet. As Mental Health Officer, it was not her position to involve herself in border politics. Even when those border politics scattered unconscious Marines all over her consulting room floor.

Rising to her feet, she walked to the door and pulled it open. Spoke quietly to the competent nurse practitioner waiting on the other side, and then returned to her chair to wait. Cecil would survive one more session with her. Ten or fifteen minutes, perhaps. She took a sip of the cold coffee she'd left beside the yellow pad and then tapped her fingers on the arm of the chair.

Five minutes later, once Cecil had been dosed and was sitting upright, if twitchy, in his own chair, Dolores resumed her conversation with him.

"How are you feeling, Cecil?"

"Where am I?"

"You're here," she replied, underlining 'short term memory loss' on the pad, "because of the incident in the truck. With the girl. And the glue. Do you remember, Cecil?"

"Uh," he vigorously rubbed his nose with the palm of his hand, "yeah."

"Good. I'm glad." She gave him a gentle look. "Can you remember what happened to the other people in the truck?"

Panicked, he gaped at the closed door. "Where's Mel?"

"He's fine, Cecil." Soothing. "Sleeping in the next room."

"Oh." He sagged into the chair. "Good."

"The others," she persisted, taking a chance, "aren't. Fine. In fact, Cecil, they're missing. Their families have begun to worry about them." She consulted her pad. "Dictys. Epopeus. Lycabas—"

"They didn't stand a chance," Cecil murmured.

"You know what's become of them?" Dolores modulated her voice. Kept the eagerness strictly out of it.

"It was the girl," he said.

"The girl?"

"She's no girl." He shook his head as vigorously as he'd been rubbing at his nose. "Not a real girl at all."

Dolores now controlled her annoyance, which had, in a split second, replaced the earlier eagerness. The conversation was going in the same inane direction it had gone fifteen times before. With both Mel and Cecil. Into the region of madness (though she didn't like to use the term professionally) and absurdity. Patient, however, she waited. Letting him finish his piece.

"No girl at all," he repeated sadly.

"Why do you say that?"

"She told us she wanted a ride in the truck, right?" His tone was pleading. Frightened.

"Yes?"

"So, we brought the truck around to collect her."

"Why did you do that?"

"Because she asked." As though it were obvious. Bewildered that she'd need to pose the question.

"I see." She underlined 'suggestible— hypnosis?' on her pad. Then she looked up at him. "Continue. You brought the truck around."

"No," he said. "Mel brough the truck around. I had the honor of keeping her protected."

"The honor?"

"Yes." His twitching had become distracting to them both, but he was as motivated as Dolores to get through the story. And so, he ignored it. "She wanted to go to the foreign quarter. You know, with the clubs? I think her pimp owns property there."

"I see." She underlined 'vice.'

"But the guys, well, they thought it would be funny to mess with her. Little girl, you know. High-handed and giving all the orders." He shuddered. "So they told Mel to head north.

66

Pretend we were selling her to the Empire. She commanded us to stop, but that just made them laugh harder. The glue, you know, had made them a little—" He didn't finish the sentence.

"I understand."

"She ordered them to stop again, and they started, like, poking at her, with their fingers—" He faltered. "Tickling, maybe? Because she was just a little girl, you know—"

"Yes?"

"She turned them into fish."

It was only Dolores's upbringing and training that kept her from lobbing the pad of paper at him. As she wanted to do every time he reached this point in the story. Instead, she took a smooth breath.

"Fish."

His mouth was working. "No, not fish. You know, great big fish. That breathe air. Dolphins. Porpoises. I don't know." He was weeping freely. "But we were on the road, right? No water. At least not that they could get to. So the guys all start changing, and they're making these sounds." He clapped his hands over his ears, shaking his head. "Awful sounds. And Mel and I could see that their eyes were the same. They were the same guys. Just—just fish. Dolphins. In a truck."

He gulped in two sobbing breaths and continued. "And then, they sort of flopped out of the back of the truck. Onto the concrete road. Most of them died when they hit. But one or two of them—" He shook his head a second time.

67

"They were still moving on the hot cement. Squirming and bleeding. Trying to get themselves to water." He paused. "She only let Mel alone because he was driving."

Dolores, fuming, underlined 'hallucination—possible psychotic break?' Otherwise, she remained pleasant, gracious, and calm. Understanding. "And what about you, Cecil? Why didn't she magically transform you into a fish?"

"A dolphin."

"A dolphin."

"She could see that I was afraid of her. Even before that." He gulped in more air. "She knew that I—that I'd follow her. Do as I'm told, right?"

"And now?"

"What now?"

"If the little girl were to give you an order now, Cecil, would you obey her?"

"She isn't a little girl," he said.

Dolores began to re-frame the question in the hope of eliciting a more useful response from him. But before she could find the words, Cecil's face began to slacken again. His eyes to lose focus. This time, in fact, his eyes clouded over for a good two or three minutes before he lost consciousness. Sleepy and staring blindly at nothing, he continued to speak, channeling, it seemed to Dolores, a sort of warning.

"Watch out for her," he slurred. "She's no little girl. You'll regret not paying her due respect."

68

Hollow. Someone else's voice.

Dolores, who had already set the pad to her side, looked up at him. "What?"

"She's more powerful than any of you," he intoned. "Watch out—"

And then he slipped to the floor.

Yet again, Dolores found herself crouching beside him, feeling for his pulse. Frustrated. More perturbed than she wanted to admit by his last few words. The girl was obviously an unhealthy presence at the Consulate. Whoever she was. And the solution to the problem was equally obviously to have her placed somewhere such that she would no longer pose the mental health threat that she was currently posing. For her own good too, of course. The Republic was well-equipped to deal with citizens in need of rehabilitation. Excellent healthcare system. Historically.

She stood and dusted off the knees of her muted, well-tailored suit. Produced for her by the same couturier that had served her mother's family for three hundred fifty years. Though no one in the Consulate—with the possible exception of the Consul General, who deliberately ignored it—had the knowledge or expertise to recognize the tailoring for what it was. She frowned and fixed a twisted cuff.

As for the warning—if that's what it had been, though she doubted it—she'd place the same value on it that she'd placed on its mouthpiece. With a lack of dignity that surprised even herself, she snorted. As though someone like Dolores would take seriously the addled ranting of some blind, half-wit addict.

"Watch out," indeed. Her obligation now was to find Rhys, detach the girl from his protection, and end this crisis permanently. It bothered Dolores that she herself was the only member of the Consular staff to see the solution with any clarity. But then, such was frequently the case. Her troubled inheritance.

RHYS and the girl were sitting at a small, round, wobbling table to the side of the food court. He was drinking a cup of coffee. The girl, sleepy and serious, was eating white powdered doughnuts from a heap towering on a plate a few inches in front of her. The pile of doughnuts reached nearly to her forehead. Though, Dolores noted with distaste, the girl was slouching. As usual.

Nodding a greeting to the young man with the rocks who was consuming a plate of what looked like calamari, she navigated her way to the girl's table. The social climbing attaché with the sunglasses had asked Dolores to look in on the man, but Dolores hadn't yet taken the opportunity. Aside from the one eccentricity—carting the rocks about with him everywhere in a deteriorating sack (three were occupying the other chairs at his table while he ate)—he seemed well enough adjusted. If talkative.

And gossip had it that his career was golden, despite the quirk—having leapt from the purgatory of Visa Services to Assistant Head of

Economic Affairs Analysis in less than a month. Whatever the case, Dolores dismissed him from her mind. She had more important issues to occupy herself at the moment.

Rhys waved to her when he saw her approaching, and Dolores smiled in turn, speeding up. She and Rhys had always got on well together. Developing a solution to the difficulty with the girl ought not be difficult. Dolores predicted they'd have her out of the Consulate and on a secure bus elsewhere—ideally somewhere cordoned off by wire—by late afternoon. Problem solved.

She pulled out a chair and sat between Rhys and the girl. The round table was small enough that she had to move her legs to the side. She did so, crossed them, and folded her hands over her knees.

"Hi Rhys."

"Hey Dolores."

She smiled at the girl. "And how do you do?" she asked in the language of the Republic.

The girl yawned at her. White powder coating her nose and chin. The stench of glue coming off of her in waves, making Dolores's eyes water. Then she reached for another doughnut and ate it. Gazed, bleary and unfocused, about the food court as she chewed.

Dolores blinked back her tears, nonplussed. The girl was wearing a floral pink dress that was too large for her, no shoes, and a plastic bag full of packages of facial tissue wedged between her thighs. She also had dirt and what

71

Dolores thought might be leaves—and possibly a moth—in her hair.

Dolores turned to Rhys. "Where are her shoes?"

"She won't wear them." He sipped his coffee. "We tried."

"You know she can't stay here."

"Why not?"

She looked at him.

"She's good for morale," he persisted. "And it isn't as though she takes up a lot of room."

"Good for morale?" She laughed at him. "Have you seen my consulting room?"

He laughed in turn. Not offended. "Collateral damage."

"And the others? The ones who've gone missing?"

"Disobedient."

"Really, Rhys," she said. "You can't be serious."

"You know what I think the problem is?" Playful and roguish, which was unlike him.

"What?"

"You're just jealous that you're not the only person related to Our Great Founder who's attached to the Consulate anymore." He grinned at her.

Dolores raised her eyebrows. "What? That girl? She doesn't even speak the language."

"A by-blow. She told us herself."

Dolores didn't ask in what language the girl had told them. Instead, she tilted her head at him, uncertain as to how much of his banter was a joke. Ordinarily, she was good at byplay of this sort—though, as a reserved person, she found it disagreeable. But his attitude now, while certainly facetious, also struck her as ever so slightly threatening.

She felt her way forward.

"Rhys," she began, "that girl is, at most, twelve years old. Our Great Founder died seventy years ago."

She paused. And then, she stopped altogether. Deciding to keep back the information, from her father, that as potent as Our Great Founder had been as a political leader, he'd been less so when it came to the biological side of nation-building. "By-blows," as Rhys had put it, were unlikely.

Rhys held his hand over his chest in the same mocking-not-mocking manner. "Our Great Founder," he declared, "lives eternally in the hearts and minds of the people."

"Yes," she said patiently, "in their hearts and in their minds. Not in their uteruses. Besides," she added with more asperity than she'd intended, "*your* founder is outside there in the wig and the buckled heels. Why are you so interested in Republican bloodlines all of a sudden?"

"And why are you such a bigot, Dolores?" His smile was definitely forced now. "Who cares if she speaks the language?"

"Look," she said, trying to placate him, "I'm not making any comment on the qualities or—

73

or the blood—of the girl. She seems a very nice girl." She tried to keep the contempt from her voice. "But it's obvious that she can't stay here. Or with you. This is a Consulate. You command the Marines. It's impossible."

"You're not putting her on a bus, Dolores." The smile was entirely gone. "No re-settlement. No re-integration." He fixed her with a cold stare. "No wire."

Dolores frowned. She hadn't remembered voicing the intention out loud. But, regrouping, she pushed ahead, moderate and persuasive. "A compromise, then." She uncrossed her legs. "I'll take her upstairs. Give her the care she needs here. On-site. You can't deny that she's got addiction problems. And we have one of the best facilities in the country." She swallowed. "I give you my word that she won't be harmed."

"Your word."

"Yes," Dolores said. "My word. She won't be harmed."

He gazed across the table at her for close to thirty seconds.

"Very well," he finally agreed.

He nodded to the girl. And the girl, who had eaten every doughnut from the plate during their exchange, reached into the plastic sack between her legs and pulled out a packet of facial tissue. Held it out to Dolores.

Rhys, grim, looked on.

"Fine," Dolores said after a split second of hesitation. Then she stood, fishing in her pocket for loose change, scooped out a few coins, and handed them to the girl.

The girl, in turn, pressed the facial tissue into Dolores's palm. After securing the coins in some hidden recess of the pink dress, she also stood. Teetered a bit. Grabbed the back of the chair to remain upright. Before holding her hand out to Dolores.

After another few seconds of now disgusted hesitation—she didn't want to touch the girl—Dolores took the offered hand and walked in the direction of the stairs. Clutching the packet of tissues in her other hand. Everyone in the food court, including the young man with the rocks, watched as they retreated from the room. As though they were part of some ritual procession. Dolores found herself shivering.

UPON reaching the clinic, however, she shook off the artificial awe that had dogged her in the food court. Once more, all she felt for the girl was revulsion. And as she well knew, both from her own training and from the Republic's history, "she won't be harmed" was a slippery phrase at best in the psychiatric-medical profession. Rhys needn't know. All sorts of things happened for a patient's own good. All sorts of things that she, Dolores, intended to sample now. Never one to miss an opportunity.

When they reached an empty consulting room—not her own, something anonymous—Dolores dropped the girl's hand and turned to a sink to wash her own, energetically, in the hottest water that she could force from the tap. Then, ignoring the girl, who was standing dazed beside a bare gurney with dangling straps, she searched through two cupboards until she found what she wanted. An ampule. A syringe. Gloves. Turning back, she locked the door to the room.

"On the examination table," she said to the girl in the language of the Republic that she, Dolores, represented.

When nothing happened, she stepped away from the door and closer to the girl. Quietly flourishing the syringe. "On the examination table," she repeated in the language of the Republic she served.

Still, the girl remained immobile. But not disobedient. Neither mocking nor mischievous. Simply inert. After a second or two, she rubbed her nose with a closed fist. Spreading the white powder further over her cheeks.

Dolores kept her temper. As she always did. Training and blood. Carefully setting the syringe on a counter beside the sink, she grabbed the girl under her arms and hoisted her onto the gurney. Tipping her partway back.

Though the girl neither struggled nor resisted, her dead weight was more than Dolores had expected. The Mental Health Officer staggered for a moment as she stepped back from the wheeled table. Felt a disquieting twinge in her lower spine.

And then she raised her eyebrows. The girl had been twelve—at a stretch, a mature eleven—when they'd entered the consulting room. Now, however, arranged on the table, she appeared closer to nineteen or twenty. And a lascivious nineteen or twenty, at that.

The floral dress was stretched tightly across her fleshy, rather than wiry, body, a size or more too small. Its stray pink threads stirred and eddied in her persistently snuffling breath. And her chest heaved up and down like the chest of a distraught romantic heroine as she took in and expelled the room's flat air. The only part of her body that *was* properly mobile.

Dolores could easily imagine the reaction that the girl, in her current state, would elicit from the unfortunate sort of men and women who found themselves attracted to wanton listlessness. To indolence. Even Dolores, who preferred sober intelligence, could feel its magnetism.

Pushing down her disgust (and interest), she returned her attention to the syringe. Doubtless the transformation—*apparent* transformation—was a trick of the light. A distortion of Dolores's own heightened emotions. Of her stress following the bewildering conversation with Rhys, whom she'd always believed to be her friend. She corrected herself: her friendly colleague. Dolores wasn't good at friendship.

Or, of course, it could be nothing more than a product of the girl's origins. It was impossible to determine the age of these street children with any reliability—they were all mature, inappropriately mature, from birth. As cunning as they were wild. She told herself to remain professional and detached. Despite her mounting irritation.

"Lie back, please." In both languages. Without looking at the girl.

She turned. The girl was not lying back. Rather, she was supporting herself on her elbows, her legs splayed, in precisely the position Dolores had left her. She snuffled two or three more times. Her breasts heaved.

Dolores took a calming breath of her own. Then, gently, she returned the syringe to the counter. After which, without speaking, she stepped toward the girl and pushed her back on the gurney until she was supine. Retrieved one of the dangling straps and secured the girl's left wrist. Circled the table, retrieved a second strap, and secured her right wrist. As she did so, the girl let out a distinctly non-medical moan.

Shocked, Dolores nearly dropped the restraint. But then, pressing her lips together, she jerked it tight. She refused to let the girl demoralize her as she completed her duty. She also refused to acknowledge the lazy smile that had crossed the girl's face when the strap had cuffed her wrist.

"This may pinch at first," Dolores informed her, returning with the syringe. "But it ought to wake you up. Get you talking."

Without further warning, she jammed the needle into the girl's upper arm. The girl neither flinched nor cried out. In fact, she reacted to the injection not at all. Her breathing remained indolent and steady. Her body relaxed.

But Dolores wasn't paying attention to irrelevant emotional or nervous responses to the treatment. Instead, watching the wall clock, she waited for the seconds hand to complete a rotation and a half. Then, satisfied that nothing untoward had occurred, she returned her scrutiny to the gurney.

And frowned again. The girl ought at least to have been flushed. Her pupils dilated. At best—and what Dolores had been expecting, given the girl's size, or, that is, her former size—was excited and anxious jerking. Twisting against the bonds. And, of course, hyperlogia. In any language. Dolores didn't care which.

But the girl remained in the same condition she'd been before. A vague smile. White powder smeared across her face. Slow, measured, lazy breathing.

Dolores pressed her fingertips against the girl's neck, feeling halfheartedly for a pulse. It was sluggish. Unaffected by the drug.

"How do you feel?" she finally asked.

"More," the girl whispered in the language of the Republic. Or, perhaps, the language of the other Republic.

It was the first word she'd spoken to Dolores, and yet oddly, despite Dolores's increasingly obsessive interest in the girl's linguistic background, its dialect was impossible to detect. Dolores felt as though the girl's voice had been inserted, injected, directly into her brain. Floating and absent origin.

"What?" she finally asked.

"It's good stuff," the girl rasped. "More. More. *More.*"

Dolores stared, cold, into the girl's eyes. "Good idea."

She retrieved a second ampule, filled the syringe, and injected the girl. Waited a minute and a half. Nothing. The girl smiled and smiled. And smiled some more.

"More," she eventually repeated.

Dolores nodded, curt, and found a third ampule. A fourth. A fifth. By the end of forty five minutes, the girl had absorbed sufficient quantities of the stimulant that her heart ought to have given out. Many times over.

And yet, it was Dolores instead whose cheeks were flushed and whose blood pressure was high. Inattentive to the broken glass scattered across the floor and to the latex clogging the sink. She'd removed her gloves after the first fifteen minutes. The better to work quickly.

It was also Dolores herself who felt close to cardiac arrest when the door to the examination room swung open. Surely, she'd locked it? Twisting back to loosen the girl's restraints— wanting to lessen the effect of the scene on external observers—she likewise failed to notice who had entered.

But the reason she failed to notice the intruder was less her own self-consciousness and more the once again altered state of the girl. Sitting upright on the gurney, free of the straps, the girl was unquestionably twelve (or, at a stretch, a mature eleven) years old. The pink dress was sloppy and loose. Her body was thin and undernourished. Her eyes sleepy. The powder on her face still prominent.

Dolores knew that she'd secured the girl's wrists into the restraints. Tightly. Too tightly, because the girl's idiot smile had bothered her. It was impossible that she could have freed herself from them, especially without leaving marks or making a noise.

But aside from the issue of the restraints, there was also the change in her body. The light in the examination room hadn't wavered. There couldn't have been any trick. No distortion. And yet, the girl was now a child. Something was badly wrong.

In the two or three seconds it took Dolores to process these new developments, the intruder made herself known.

"Forgive me, Doctor." It was the nurse practitioner. Dolores's favorite nurse practitioner. "I've been sent to inform you that the girl's guardian has turned up, requesting her release."

Dolores, her heart racing, but otherwise externally under control, nodded. The nurse had said "guardian," in the same way that she would have said "pedophile" under less professional circumstances. She was no more pleased by the thought of handing the child over to him than Dolores herself was—though likely for different reasons.

But the Consulate couldn't afford to start a war with the Republic's underworld. Indeed, Consular policy was that the underworld didn't exist at all. No one saw it. And its periodic eruptions were explained away as freak accidents. Keeping the girl wasn't worth shattering the fragile, never verbalized peace that every Consular official daily maintained in covert and silent vigilance.

And so, the girl slithered off the gurney and approached the nurse. Tripping slightly over a crushed ampule. As she walked, she gazed up at Dolores.

"You're crazy fun," she rasped. "Party tonight. Lots of boys. Girls too. Whatever you want. See you there—"

Her knees buckled and she began to crumple into a giggling heap, but the nurse practitioner efficiently heaved her upright and helped her from the room. Exchanging a pained glance with Dolores as she shut the door. Well understanding the trials that the Mental Health Officer faced when dealing with bureaucratic ineptitude.

Dolores nodded her gratitude as the door closed. The nurse practitioner often felt like a

mother to her. She was lucky to have such a
capable person serving alongside her.

Then she turned back to the wheeled bed.
The girl had left something behind as she'd
slinked away. In her wake. A rectangle of paper in
a pool of sweat, it looked to be. Dolores narrowed
her eyes and examined it more closely. A calling
card. She lifted it. Coated in honey rather than in
sweat.

Revolted, she dropped it to the counter and
pulled on clean latex gloves. Pushing the mystery
of where the honey had originated from her mind.
Irrelevant. And disturbing.

More important was the card. Otherwise
blank, it listed the name and address of one of the
roving clubs that had made the former
ambassadorial neighborhood globally notorious.
Tonight's address, that is. Roving as they were,
their locations always changed. There was also a
tiny, stylized ivy leaf in the upper left corner of the
frayed paper. And what may have been a snake.

She'd ignore it, obviously. Excessive
knowledge of the practices of those infected by the
vice that the street children had introduced to the
Consulate might compromise her professional
objectivity. Better to keep a distance. Better not to
know. Certainly, she'd ignore it.

DOLORES reached the abandoned
coffee shop in which the party was being held at
five minutes to midnight. Not a real coffee shop, of
course. One of millions of identical outposts of a

global coffee-shop empire, it had, until two months before, towered four storeys above the mid-nineteenth-century residential buildings that had transfigured what had once been a closed and intricate medieval village. Clean, efficient, and desperately eager to please.

That is, the imperial coffee-shop outpost had been clean, efficient, and desperately eager to please until the militant Greens had gutted and set fire to it. Scrawling graffiti against the backdrop of the conflagration touting the superiority of Nescafé. Now, the building was a ruin, and the leaders and representatives of the global coffee-shop empire were determining whether restoring it was worth the money that would need to be spent on public relations. Keeping the Greens off of it for a few more months.

In its reincarnation as a setting for the roving party, the building had, Dolores felt as she observed it, come into its own. Its exterior windows, which had been blacked out and draped with paperboard, reverberated visibly to the music inside. And anyone passing who neared the scorched walls could hear—and feel—the edifice shuddering as they passed. One merely had to remain conscious of the vibrations of the medieval cobblestones and the nineteenth-century concrete as one wandered by to be made aware that something wondrous was happening inside.

She smoothed the front of the blue sheath she'd worn to blend in with the revelers. Absentminded. It came from the same couturier that produced most of her tailoring, and Dolores knew instinctively that it was flawless. Sartorial issues rarely concerned her.

More worrisome was her need for anonymity. As she hesitated outside, she remained uncertain as to how she would enter the place without immediately drawing the unwelcome attention of its regulars to her anomalous presence. Not to mention its new, and newly addicted, visitors from the Consulate.

For Dolores had taken up the girl's invitation for two reasons, and two reasons alone: first, she believed that knowledge of the enemy would help her to counsel her patients; and second, she half-hoped to encounter at least a few of the missing Marines. Third, she was curious. But she refused to acknowledge the curiosity.

What she did not need, consequently, was to be swarmed by delighted and potentially intoxicated colleagues from the Consulate when they noticed her arrival. She wasn't one of them. Her concern, quite the contrary, was to extract and to cure them.

As it happened, however, Dolores needn't have feared for her anonymity. From the moment she entered the abandoned coffee shop, it was clear that not a single participant in the celebration was intellectually capable of identifying her. Even in the dark strobing light, she could see that their pupils were dilated beyond anything she'd ever encountered. And though their dancing was frenetic, their faces were slack. A few drooled or chewed ferociously on plastic teething rings. The smell of glue was overpowering. There would, she quickly concluded, be no awkward conversation.

In fact, less than two minutes after she'd entered, she was ready to leave. She'd witnessed enough. More than enough. She'd arrange a conversation with the Consul General tomorrow morning about opening negotiations with the officially nonexistent underworld. Demand its rulers leave their people alone. And, above all, block the street children from Consular grounds. It was the street children, the girl, who were the thin edge of the wedge—

"Is it a fish?"

Dolores whipped her head around. The voice was coming from just above her. Rhys. He'd propelled himself, somehow, from the upper storey to the second, where she stood looking down at the horror that was the dance floor. Now, he staggered toward her, gnawing on an orange ring that was squirting out whatever liquid had once filled it. Staring, fixated, at her dress.

She glanced down at the material. The blue, she noticed, was picking up the strobe lights in an unusual way. Blinking and flowing. Looking, perhaps, like a fish—

"Not a fish. A dolphin."

Startled, she turned to her right. Cecil. Draped over Mel. Though how they'd escaped the clinic she couldn't fathom. Also, they were naked. And they'd painted their penises with rainbow glitter. Dolores flushed and lowered her eyes.

"Here, fish, fish fish—"

"Dolphin!" With a violent heave, Cecil tossed Mel over the edge of the open gallery and watched him hit the floor. "Bye, bye."

She swallowed. "Hi Rhys. Interesting party."

Rather than responding, he reached out and pawed at her dress. "Is it a fish?"

"Look," she continued, "this isn't really my scene—"

"And what happens to a fish?"

Dolores widened her eyes at the voice, gagging when she confirmed its source. "Jesus Christ."

It was the nurse practitioner. Wearing, however, a naughty nurse outfit that looked direct from a pornographic supplier. At least three sizes too small.

"We stick it." The nurse pulled an enormous syringe from some impossible place in her outfit. "That's what we do with a fish. We *stick* it."

"Oh God." Dolores turned to escape, but Rhys grabbed her by the arms and held her in place.

"Stick the fish," he said.

"Stick it."

Various other party goers had crowded, dazed, around the commotion, and they too were rubbing their hands against her dress and muttering or shouting about sticking the fish.

Dolores tried to speak further. But before the words could come, the nurse had rammed the needle into her neck. A few seconds later, she also felt injection points in her arms, thighs, and buttocks. Countless different needles insinuating themselves under her skin. In her fear and confusion, she even imagined one or two being wielded by the rocks owned by the Assistant Head of Economic Affairs Analysis. On their own unsympathetic initiative.

But the pain, mercifully, lasted for less than a minute. Sinking to the floor, she quickly felt a clean and icy euphoria flooding her brain, replacing the agony and the terror. Moreover, gazing spellbound at the material of her dress, she decided that, yes, it did resemble the skin of a fish. Intrigued, she prodded at it with her fingers.

No. Not a fish. A dolphin. And not resemble. Dolores herself had become a dolphin. Was in the process of becoming a dolphin. The eternal dolphin, she giggled to herself. Thinking of Heidegger. Who had a very silly name. Her situation had nothing to do with her dress. Indeed, she couldn't even find the dress any longer.

Regretting her earlier lack of sympathy, she tried to locate Cecil instead to indicate to him that she finally understood his story about the missing Marines. To tell him that he'd been correct, and that she now believed him. That the girl was no girl, and that she'd turned the disobedient soldiers into fish. Dolphins.

But, as a dolphin, she quickly discerned that movement through the coffee shop was difficult. As was speech. As, oddly, was breathing.

But didn't dolphins breathe air? She panicked.

The moment of panic at the respiration situation, however, dissipated in an instant when she realized to her relief that Rhys, Cecil, Mel (who had returned from the floor below, apparently unharmed), the nurse practitioner, the Assistant Head of Economic Affairs Analysis, his rocks, the Consul General, and several other celebrants—including, she was gratified to note, many of the missing Marines—were looking after her non-dolphin body parts for safe keeping. Seeing to it that she didn't misplace them.

Rhys, for example, was holding up a bloody leg. Waving it about like a flag. Though the flag of which Republic, she couldn't determine. One or the other. She must ask him later.

Cecil had replaced the rubber duck he'd been chewing before with her elbow. Masticating it into a shredded pink pulp. While Mel held her two hands, severed at the wrists, and clapped them together. And the nurse practitioner brandished her head on a stick.

Dolores wondered for a moment how she, Dolores, could see the nurse practitioner displaying her head, given that her eyes were embedded in it at the top of the stick. But then Rhys, always her good friend, reached up with a thumb and forefinger, plucked first one eye, and then the other, out of the head, and swallowed them both. Which solved the problem.

In the blind blackness, Dolores repeated to herself that, as a dolphin, it really was terribly difficult to breathe in an environment like an abandoned, non-watery coffee shop. More than enough time to learn, however. An eternity, really.

She also decided that she very much liked the smell of glue.

CHARIOT

THE black stretch Cadillac SUV sparkled in the sunlight. But Apan wasn't looking at it. Instead, he was watching his father. Polishing it. Caring for it. Even in his illness. The Cadillac, as Apan and his family all knew but didn't acknowledge, was killing his father, who operated it on behalf of the ghouls who inhabited the fortress. Day and night, never ceasing, never resting. His father wouldn't last much longer. Yes still, he drove. It was a job.

Apan's family had once lived prosperously, flourishing in the suburb that the fortress had crushed. Not anymore. Now, they no longer existed. Officially. But rather than fighting or denouncing or even subverting the injustice, Apan's father had reacted to the catastrophe by taking piecemeal work from the monsters who had ruined them. Tempted not only by the promise of food, shelter, and a regular income, but by the more tantalizing possibility—always implied rather than made explicit—of visas for himself and his family. Provided, of course, that he never shirked his duty. That he never, ever stopped.

Apan had been old enough when the calamity had fallen not to question his father's accommodation of the ghouls. And in the intervening years, he'd seen what had happened to those who had fought or denounced or subverted them. He by no means resented or regretted his family's precarious position at the edge of the Consulate's protective shadow. His mother on occasion even boasted about it. Though Apan wished that she wouldn't. For reasons of etiquette, if nothing else.

Nonetheless, he couldn't entirely suppress his bitterness whenever he watched his father killing himself to care for the hulking conveyance in which he transported his masters. He might at least have dawdled. Protested his impossible position via the occasional slapdash waxing of the thing.

"Effie called me a traitor today." He hadn't meant to say anything to his father. But the sight of the old man groveling beneath the wheel well of the SUV had forced the words from his mouth.

"And you ignored him, didn't you?" His father's voice was muffled. He was cleaning a spot of dust from the silver ridge of a back wheel.

Apan clenched his hands into fists. He was seventeen, still wearing the uniform of the school he attended on the back of his parents' daily sacrifice. "Maybe I am a traitor."

"Traitors are political," his father replied. "One way or the other. We're not. We're decent. We work hard. That's all."

"For what?" Apan wished he could stop talking. He didn't know what perversity was prompting him to extend the exchange.

"You know what."

"Money."

"More than money. Visas."

"Effie says you're a fool." Apan could scarcely believe he was saying these things to his father. But, unable to check himself, he continued. "He says they use you."

His father chuckled. "If Effie could hear what I hear every day, he'd know who was a fool."

"I want to hear it."

His father was silent for three or four seconds. And then he pulled himself out from under the Cadillac. Ran his hands over the dirt and oil that had accumulated on his work shirt. Began to stand, but staggered before he was fully upright.

Apan ran over to help him. Held his shoulders as his father coughed into a handkerchief. Was briefly overwhelmed by guilt at having questioned him, tired him, at all.

"What do you mean," his father asked when he was standing straight, his voice under control, "that you want to hear it?"

Now that it was out, Apan was determined to make his case. "I'm seventeen. I can drive as well as you can. You need a rest. I've never seen you take a day off." He paused. "I can help."

"Now who's a fool?"

"I can help," he insisted. "And I want to hear."

His father studied him. His earnest face.

"No," he eventually said. "You're not a fool. You're a lunatic. Have you any idea what happens in that vehicle?"

"I don't," Apan admitted. "But I want to. I'm old enough. Besides," he added artfully, "we'll want to keep the position—the job—in the family, right? For the visas?"

"A lunatic," his father repeated, "but not a fool." He lowered himself onto a chair at the edge of the garage. "No one but me can drive that Cadillac. No one. Not even Our Great Founder."

"Our Great Founder," Apan replied, "would have known better than to ruin himself performing the same task day after day until his body and mind fell to pieces around him. Father, you can't go on. And if I prove myself, we'll relieve one another. Take rests. All I'm asking is one day."

"One day, and then you'll stop pestering me?"

"One day," Apan affirmed.

His father closed his eyes. "Very well. Tomorrow. May as well get this nonsense out of your head quickly."

He forced open his lids, gummy from sleep deprivation and exertion, and stared across the garage at his son. "But you'll do exactly as I tell you, you hear?"

94

Apan nodded.

His father cogitated for close to a minute. Dissatisfied, but unable to summon up an argument that would persuade his son to drop the appeal. And then, abruptly, he spoke again.

"First," he said, "you'll arrive in front of building, to the east of the founders sculpture, at 6:30 in the morning. Exactly at 6:30. No earlier. No later."

"I understand."

"Good." His father looked more than pained now. Pale. Shivering. But still, he continued. "Second, you'll drive wherever they command you to drive without hesitating and without asking questions. No matter how bizarre the request, you'll do what they tell you. You don't refuse. You don't speak to them."

"Yes."

"And third," his father finished, as though rushing to get through it before changing his mind, "most important of all: don't look back. You'll collect passengers along the way. When that happens, you'll slow when they tell you to slow, stop when they tell you to stop, and then keep your eyes straight ahead as the passengers enter and exit the vehicle."

"I understand."

"Never, ever," his father emphasized, "look in the mirror."

"Okay." A bit less confident.

"You pay attention to me, boy. *Never* look in the mirror. Straight ahead. Stay on course. Go where you're told. Arrive on time." His father inhaled a rattling lungful of air. "You keep yourself to yourself, and if you must occupy your mind with the job, consider the condition of the Cadillac. Never the passengers. Imagine cleaning it. Waxing it. Caring for it. Nothing else."

"I understand."

"Good. Fine." His father shooed him out of the garage. "Now go and tell your mother to bring me a glass of water."

APAN had the Cadillac waiting at the doors of the Consulate, spruce and shining, just as the clock on the dash was switching from 6:29 to 6:30. His father's uniform fit him perfectly. And his keyed up energy was suppressed—viciously—under a veneer of cool professionalism. He was prepared.

At 6:32, a frumpy woman wearing unnecessary sunglasses exited the building, approached the vehicle, and climbed into the passenger's seat beside him. If she noticed that he wasn't his father, she said nothing about it. Instead, with a nod, she indicated that they ought to move.

It was only once he'd driven them onto the shore road leading from the Consulate's suburb to the interior of the city that she spoke. Terse and close to inaudible. Almost to herself. Though in Apan's language.

"The Four Seasons Hotel."

He nodded and maneuvered the Cadillac onto the ramp that would dump them, twenty minutes later, in front of the hotel. And at 6:54, he pulled the SUV into position. Satisfied by his work, even if the woman wasn't acknowledging it.

When they rolled to a stop, their passenger was already waiting outside on the pavement, to the left of a hovering porter. At a gesture from the figure, the porter opened the rear door, and a middle-aged professional woman stepped up and arranged herself at the edge of one of the two back seats that were longer than was conventional, and that were designed to face one another. Shingled hair. Severe spectacles. Equally severe skirt suit.

Apan, who had already forgotten his father's injunction against looking in the mirror, recognized her as one of the more charismatic of the Republic's parliamentarians. He'd seen her frequently on their family's hijacked television haranguing crowds and cutting down political opponents with three or four barbed and well-chosen words. Having built her career on campaigning, sometimes militantly, against corruption and vice, she was popularly presumed to be the country's next Prime Minister. She opened a file she'd brought into the car with her, straightened her spectacles, and began to read.

Chewing his bottom lip and pushing down the Cadillac's accelerator with a touch too much force, Apan began to drive in the direction of their next destination. The woman with the sunglasses had been compelled to speak twice before he'd moved. Intrigued, he hadn't heard her the first time. And now, irritated with himself for his brief dereliction of duty, he was already flustered.

Perhaps, Apan thought as he brought them toward the highway, this was why his father had ordered him not to look back. Less fear for what he might see in the rear of the Cadillac and more concern that he'd become interested and fail to follow orders as quickly as he ought to. Either way, Apan was disappointed. Though the MP was impressive, she was hardly stupefying—and, more to the point, she was by no means the sort of passenger to quiet his friend Effie's hints that Apan's father was a stooge. Thus far, Apan was having difficulty understanding his father's near sacerdotal reverence for doing his job and *only* his job until the very day, minute, and second that it killed him. It all seemed so trivial.

Their next stop was an ostentatious free-standing bungalow in an expensive gated community overlooking the water. As they slowed, Apan could see, from their position beside the house, an aircraft carrier from the north squeezing its way through the channel and toward the shipping lanes. It was now 7:22. But they were obliged to wait for six and a half minutes until their passenger appeared.

When he did appear, portly, unshaven, and out of uniform, Apan was once more surprised. But also, once more, disappointed. The city's Chief of Police. Well known to be on the payroll of several leaders of the Republic's informal economy—and a close friend of that neighboring monarch's nephew who was at the center of all the salacious rumors—he was certainly an odd companion for the anti-corruption minister to keep with her in the back of a car. Yet again, however, Apan was by no means awestruck or confounded by his presence. He, too, wasn't worth his family's imminent disintegration.

He flicked his eyes to the mirror to watch the man heave himself into the back seat of the Cadillac. Feeling little guilt or hesitation this time—his father's warnings having already dwindled to a minor irritation at the corner of his mind. And when the woman with the sunglasses gave him his next order, he heard her without needing a repetition. Neither the MP nor the Chief were fatally important enough to Apan to occupy his entire attention.

Apan continued glancing at the passengers as he drove them away from the man's bungalow. The MP, he observed, read her file, ignoring the Chief of the Police. And the Chief of Police, who had taken the position on the other end of the long seat, also facing forward, closed his eyes as though in pain. Or, Apan decided, after another quick look, hung over.

Less compelled than he thought he'd be, Apan drove on. Their third destination was less than five minutes away, a bungalow in the same community. But they waited less than thirty seconds for their passenger. At 7:29, clean, nicely dressed, and—as Apan soon discovered—reeking of aftershave, a popular and rabidly nationalist talk show host jogged down the steps of his terraced garden, waving to his wife who stood in the doorway, and then pulled himself up and into the Cadillac.

He chose the empty seat facing backward. Sat in the middle, halfway between the MP and the Chief of Police. Without speaking, he inserted ear buds and fiddled with something in the pocket of his suitcoat. Two or three seconds later, Apan heard the tinny echo of something by ABBA. *Dancing Queen.*

Frowning, Apan waited for his next set of instructions. He'd seen the talk show host on the television as well—indeed, it was difficult for anyone living and conscious in the Republic to avoid the man's image and voice—but not as frequently as he'd seen the MP. Whenever the man invaded their set, his mother switched it off. A worried frown between her eyebrows. Apan had never known why.

He crushed the memory. Instead, nodding at the murmured command of the woman with the sunglasses, he maneuvered the Cadillac in the direction of their next stop. This one was less straightforward than the first three had been. A set of coordinates on the SUV's navigation system, it turned out—after more than an hour of difficult driving—to be a dry and empty spot of shimmering dirt to the side of a deserted back road.

To reach it, Apan had driven the Cadillac first through slums, then through half-completed construction projects that would never be

finished—tax shelters for the owners of the
properties—and then onto a gravel path that wound
through an unhealthy bit of sterile ground, devoid
of the smallest hint of vegetation. Apan was
sweating by the time he brought the vehicle to a
halt at 9:06. Wondering whether this was one of
those unmentionable places of which he'd always
known but never spoken, where—things—were
tested. If so, he vowed to forget he'd seen it.
People aware of such places tended not to last very
long in the Republic.

He didn't wonder for more than a few
seconds, however, Before he'd even considered
cutting the motor or blocking out the coordinates
that shrieked to him from the navigation panel,
threatening to sear themselves into his brain
regardless of his inclinations, a thin, diseased-
looking figure began hobbling out of the glittering
nothingness and in the direction of the SUV. He
squinted out the windscreen. Not diseased. But
yes, far too thin. Wearing strapped stilettos, a white
minidress made of some sort of rubber, and a
fluffy pink bow in her copious, dyed hair.

This time, Apan did drop his eyes. He was
seventeen. He knew what she was. He'd even
furtively purchased a few magazines advertising
photos of women like her. But he'd never been
near one in the flesh. And it certainly had never
occurred to him that his upstanding father's
profession would bring him into contact with one.

He licked his dry lips as the Chief of
Police, his eyes still pained and closed, pushed

open the door on his side of the SUV. The woman, tossing him a hostile look, clamored up and over him. Rather than interacting with, or ministering to, the Chief, however, she instead knelt on the floor in front of the anti-corruption minister, pushed up the minister's skirt, and wedged her face between the minister's thighs.

Though the minister shifted a few inches to the right to facilitate the woman's work, otherwise she didn't acknowledge the addition to the cabin. Frowning slightly, she continued her perusal of the file she'd opened upon entering the Cadillac. Her breath coming a hint more quickly than it had before.

The Chief of Police, having slammed the door shut, likewise ignored the woman. And the nationalist talk show host remained a slave to ABBA. *Dancing Queen* had long since given way to *Dum Dum Diddle.*

But Apan, unlike the others, couldn't keep from staring into the mirror at the scene unfolding behind him. Mesmerized. Indeed, the woman with the sunglasses was clearing her throat, irritated, before he realized that he'd heard nothing of her next instructions. Which, it appeared, she wasn't repeating this time.

Apan, however, wasn't allowed to question her. To ask for a restatement. His father had emphasized that under no circumstances was he to speak to the occupants of the SUV. And so, for a full three seconds, he sat paralyzed.

Until, panicky and uncertain—not to mention worried about disturbing, or possibly damaging, the passengers in the back—he started off again. Slowly picking up speed, driving further and further along the barren dirt and gravel road they'd already travelled. His palms oozing sweat as they clutched the wheel.

It was only after he'd accelerated to a bumping forty miles per hour, twelve minutes into the drive, that the woman with the sunglasses snapped at him to turn back. Startled by both her voice and her obvious anger, Apan spun the wheel quickly, without thinking. And the Cadillac, with a sickening lurch, teetered on the verge of rolling, before—to Apan's near-tearful relief—righting itself with a bouncing thud.

Cringing, he checked the mirror—though he knew he ought simply to forget it existed. The passengers were unaffected. All in the same positions they'd occupied before. And the woman with the sunglasses was instructing him in a low, threatening sort of growl to move them immediately to their subsequent destination. This time, if barely, he heard and retained the information.

A dockyard. One of many departure points for the Republic's internationally renowned fencing wire. And a significant distance from the sterile gravel where the woman in the rubber dress had joined them.

In fact, the clock was moving past 10:23 when Apan wedged the SUV between two

anonymous shipping containers to wait for their
next passenger. But they didn't wait long. At 10:25,
a figure emerged from a small dinghy and climbed
up a ladder that sank into the oily water that
lapped the dock only a few feet beyond the
Cadillac's front wheels. A bandana tied over his
forehead. A deep scar along his chin. Wearing
military boots that had been produced in the
empire to the north and a military uniform
cobbled together—ironically—from material
produced by the Republic for which Apan was
currently driving.

Without thinking, Apan sucked in his
breath. This one he knew immediately. This one,
regardless of the danger, he and his friends all
hero-worshipped. It was the second in command
of the anti-Republican peasant army that
controlled at present much of the Republic's most
strategic border. In person. Less than ten feet away
from him, Apan. One of the most wanted
terrorists in the region.

When indistinct images of this man
appeared on his family's television set, his mother
increased rather than decreasing the volume,
stopped what she was doing, and smiled. Apan still
didn't know why. But he did know that the man
was making a terrible mistake entering a vehicle
that already carried an influential MP, the second
city's Chief of Police, and a professional
propagandist like the talk show host. Never mind
whatever the woman with the sunglasses was.

He felt an obscure desire to leap from the driver's seat and warn the man away. Which he suppressed immediately. His father would die should he learn that his son had taken such a step. Physically and physiologically die. Apan had no doubt. He owed it to his family to control himself.

This determination, however, didn't prevent him from accidentally releasing the Cadillac's hand brake as he watched the man approach, thereby nearly catapulting the vehicle off the edge of the dock and into the glistening industrial water. It was only the woman with the sunglasses—pulling up the brake on her own quick initiative—that saved them. Apan stared straight ahead. Too terrified to meet her eye. Not that he could meet her eye, behind the opaque lenses.

But the rebel leader appeared unperturbed by the jerking movement of the vehicle. After hoisting himself into the back, he used two hands to shift the hips of the woman who was still working on the MP, ducked to avoid hitting his head, and sank into the seat beside the talk show host. Unwinding the bandana and shoving it into a pocket.

As Apan slowly backed the Cadillac away from the edge of the dock, the rebel leader reached into another of his many pockets and extracted a book of matches and a package of cigarettes. Tapping out two of the latter, he offered one to the talk show host. Gauloises, Apan noted irrelevantly.

"Thanks." The talk show host leant forward to allow the rebel leader to light the cigarette for him.

"No worries." The rebel leader lit his own and relaxed into his seat.

A few seconds later, the talk show host offered him one of his earbuds. Smiling, the rebel leader accepted it. Apan heard the opening strains of *Waterloo.*

The woman with the sunglasses gave him a final destination, which he both heard and retained, notwithstanding his damp hands and dry mouth. But traffic had become heavy in the city, and so Apan reached the coordinates—a youth hostel on the edge of the foreign district—at precisely noon. Moreover, though he tried to retain a fragment of control over the Cadillac, it was pure good luck that they made it there at all.

For the ongoing and distracting activities of the woman servicing the anti-corruption MP and the conviviality between the nationalist talk show host and the rebel leader—the latter of whom had opened a bottle of peasant rotgut that the two were sharing—meant that Apan couldn't tear his eyes from the mirror. Well over half of the time he drove, he did so looking behind him, and thus running the SUV over barriers, swerving into oncoming traffic, and at one point screeching along the edge of a concrete wall that had been built to keep vehicles from plunging beyond it into the sea. He knew there must be a gash now in the driver's side door that no amount of waxing would ever

106

ameliorate. And in one still unaffected part of his mind, he dreaded his father's reaction to it.

But mostly, Apan simply stared. Wrenching his eyes from the scene was beyond his control. He wasn't strong enough to ignore the figures in the back seats. And besides, he told himself with what he knew was craven selfishness, none of his passengers appeared to be disturbed in the least by his erratic driving. The five people behind him were occupied solely—and intensely—with one another. Whereas the woman with the sunglasses couldn't have been less troubled by the state of the vehicle had she been made of stone. Aside from barking periodic instructions at him, she noticed him not at all.

When Apan recognized the man who was swaggering out of the flimsy doors of the youth hostel, however, he himself turned to the woman. Sickened and astonished. He couldn't believe that, as a representative of the country she ostensibly served, the woman with the sunglasses would have any intercourse at all with this person. That any of his passengers would. Even the rebel leader.

Indeed, if the rebel leader was among the most wanted men in the region, this man was one of the most wanted men in the world. An assassin. A sadist. A trafficker and a torturer. Interpol, had they been aware of his location, would have been swarming the place.

Particularly notorious for having attempted to hijack the Popemobile—inclusive of the Pope—during a rare visit of the latter to the second city of

107

the proudly atheistic Republic, he was best known locally as the ever elusive, personal target of the city's Chief of Police. A sort of Republican Robin Hood, had Robin Hood moonlighted in acid attacks and the slave trade. And yet, as the assassin shoved himself aggressively into the back of the SUV, using a foot to shift the kneeling woman out of his way, the Chief of Police showed no reaction.

Or, that is to say, the Chief of Police opened one eye, emitted a contemptuous grunt, and settled himself back into half sleep. While the assassin, squeezing himself between the rebel leader and the talk show host, scrutinized the latter's cigarette. Less amiable than he'd been before, the rebel leader flicked a third cigarette out of the package for the assassin. Lit it.

"I said, 'drive!'"

Apan jumped. He'd failed to take in the destination again. And he didn't want to risk a recurrence of the near-rollover on the dirt road. Without speaking, he turned his eyes, politely hopeful, in the direction of the woman with the sunglasses. Silently pleading with her to repeat herself.

"Anywhere," she said after a few seconds of disgusted reticence. "Drive anywhere. We've got a full load. Two hours."

He blinked. Glanced in the mirror at the scene in the back. And admitted to himself that he was now addicted. Should he tear his eyes away from the view, he'd suffer intolerable withdrawal symptoms. Indeed, Apan barely noticed when he ran over a newspaper stand as he brought the SUV onto a wider road, away from the youth hostel. Far more important than the destruction he was causing was keeping up with the activities behind him. Watching it all unfold. Catch fire.

Once on the road, however, Apan did collect himself sufficiently to consider his options. She'd said anywhere. Two hours of anywhere. Two hours of the volatile manipulation of a vehicle over which he was decreasingly in control. Two hours of courting death.

The safest and the easiest course, he determined after a few seconds of thought, would be to drive the Cadillac for a little over an hour straight north up the empty, cliffside shore road. And then to turn back, driving due south, for another hour. If the woman with the sunglasses wanted something more elaborate, doubtless she'd tell him.

But as he drove, the woman said nothing. The people in the back continued to command his attention. And Apan, fascinated, allowed the vehicle to career wildly over and across the concrete, while the concrete became gradually free of obstacles the further north they progressed. The cliff edge steeper and more precarious.

Until, having taken a narrow curve with almost—but not quite—fatal speed, the woman ordered Apan to stop. Once he'd done so, she herself exited the Cadillac and, speaking to him through the window, indicated a ridge a half mile or so beyond where they'd halted. Apan, she said, was to drive the SUV to the ridge, wait for five minutes, return, and then collect her. After that, they'd go home.

The woman with the sunglasses then paused, waiting for the nod indicating his understanding. Which never came because Apan was too entranced by the mirror. She repeated her instructions. Apan failed to respond.

Without anger or irritation, the woman reached through the window to the ceiling of the car, grabbed the mirror, twisted it, and yanked it out of its position. Unperturbed. Then she tossed it to the floor at Apan's feet.

"Do you understand?" she repeated.

This time, he nodded. Not questioning. As his father had commanded him to do. Though it was, when he thought about it—for no more than a split second because he was mourning the mirror— a strange set of instructions.

"Good." She stepped back from the window to the rockier ground at the edge of the cliff. Gestured to him to move.

And Apan did try to drive carefully. He did try to maneuver the Cadillac responsibly. But inevitably, his desire to watch overwhelmed any desire he may once have felt for safety. For responsibility. He was, he acknowledged one last time, an addict. He couldn't help himself.

Taking a chance, therefore, he bent over and felt along the floor for the mirror. Releasing the pressure on the accelerator a bit, but not entirely. Until, pleased by his good luck, he felt his fingertips brush the edge of the glass. He had it. All he need do was affix it to the ceiling and then complete the tasks set him by the woman with the sunglasses. After that, he was free.

As Apan straightened in his seat, however, he recognized his folly. And caroming over the side of the cliff, the Cadillac somersaulted twice before landing in a flaming heap on the narrow beach. Everyone in the back died on impact. There was little chance that they'd have survived.

APAN didn't die. But he would, very soon. As he pulled himself from the wreckage, clutching the remains of the mirror, his skin burnt and shriveled, both legs and all of his ribs broken, he could just make out the woman with the sunglasses picking her way down the cliff face. Looking more preoccupied than horrified. Bored, perhaps.

After that, he lost consciousness for five or six minutes. And when he woke once more to pain and to the sickening awareness of imminent mortality, she was crouching in front of him. Poking at his smoldering uniform with curious fingertips. Possibly in an attempt to comfort him.

"Thanks, Apan," she said in his language when his eyes were open. "You've done well."

He made a noise. He wasn't certain what it meant.

"Don't worry." She patted him awkwardly on a charred shoulder. "Your father will be proud of you. And I'll try to remember to speak with Visa

111

Services tomorrow. If they aren't too busy, that is. Not long now, right?"

She stood, and Apan watched as she began to clamber up to the cliff road. Ungainly in the ugly suit. The wrong outfit for a woodland hike.

Then he closed his eyes for a last time. Apologizing to his father for the state of the Cadillac. The wax he'd need to apply to cover the damage—but then, Apan didn't want to think about that. And so, he didn't.

MEAT

KURT, the Consul General, felt
sometimes that the Exchange Program had
mobilized a deliberate and vicious vendetta against
him. He understood, of course, its position. Both
the Republic and the city in which he served were
attractive—essential window dressing for the
massive, untaxed foundation that lurked, iceberg-
like (if icebergs had shop windows), beneath the
elegant floating edifice that was the Program in
International Tolerance (its formal moniker). The
Republic and the city were jewels in the
foundation's imperial crown of charitable
education. Linchpins in the delicate balancing act it
performed between intercultural interaction and
revenue- (but never "profit"-) producing finance.
They were indispensable to the Program's
endeavors. Kurt mixed metaphors a lot.

The Republic, for example, was just
sufficiently authoritarian, teetering just close
enough to the edge of exotic, to be safe without
being embarrassing, adventurous without being
depressing. The parents and their exchanged

offspring could agree on it as a setting for the latter to lose their innocence or, if that was already gone, at least their virginity. It wasn't France. But it also wasn't Chad.

And as for the city—well, no one with a map and an internet connection would choose, upon selecting the Republic itself as a destination, to spend six to eighteen months on the empty, frigid plateau, when the cosmopolitanism, the drug culture, the easily condemned history of violence (always an attraction to the thoughtful sort of students who found themselves funded by the Program), and the myriad options in bondage offered by the second city beckoned. And obviously the capital city and the second city were the only two viable exchange locations. The borderland agricultural regions, with their resettlements and their re-integrations, their rare-earth metal extractions and their inventive modes of energy production, were best not discovered, explored, appreciated, tolerated, understood, or, for that matter, seen at all.

All of which meant that, yes, Kurt had known from the beginning of his posting that a significant portion of his time in office would be spent welcoming the bright-eyed students and massaging the dull-eyed donors—while occasionally pulling the one or the other out of embarrassments involving the marauding nephew of that tiresome neighboring Princelet. But the Exchange Program receptions, he felt, had been verging on the hysterical in recent months. He'd been forced to attend one nearly every week since the turn of the year. Two this past week.

As a result, he hadn't been out on the *Oppenheimer* for ages. Which distressed him. Because Kurt missed the *Oppenheimer*. He missed the roiling wake of the oil tankers. He missed the crew, with whom—because they shared no common language—he got on well. He also missed the food.

He particularly missed the food because, though he tried to hide it from both his acquaintances and his staff, he harbored a shameful food-related secret. The sad reality of his position at the apex of the Consular hierarchy was that his sole joy, in the whole of the time he spent representing his country to the watching Republic, was cooking in preparation for jaunts on the *Oppenheimer*. Taking advantage of the Consulate's extensive kitchens.

Indeed, Kurt adored cooking. And, though he tried not to boast, he was an excellent cook. He threw lavish dinner parties on the little boat for which he supplied the food, and to which select assortments of Consular functionaries were invited (which exposed his secret somewhat). His employees were afraid to decline the invitations, and so the Consul General's floating banquets had become a byword among the whispering entry-level officers for sacrifice in the name of duty.

Sacrifice. Duty. The dinners were, beyond question, representative of both. For whereas the Republic's cuisine, heavy on the creative use of internal organs—the end product of millennia of bellicose, mutually antagonistic populations slaughtering one another—was precisely the sort of fare to appeal to Kurt's inventive style, it was also the sort to terrorize a Consular staff used to the meat of their homeland, which for well over a century had been sufficiently divorced from its origins in field, lake, or meadow to be unrecognizable. Kurt found the disconnect between the two educational. His guests found it nauseating.

Given the relative hierarchical positions of host and guests, however, the latter nonetheless tried to be supportive of the former's efforts. As much as possible they applauded the fact that the first and only word that Kurt had learned in the local language described a soup made from the intestines of fetal sheep—a word that differed by only one letter from the Republic's word for "torture." Meaning, of course, that Kurt actually knew two words. He tried not to mix them up when interacting with the crew of the *Oppenheimer.*

Delighted by his linguistic discovery, however, Kurt had found himself just a few weeks later in a diplomatic embarrassment far more serious than accidentally threatening a crew of expendable menials with medieval interrogation tactics. While serving his own variation on the soup during a sunset cruise with the Mental Health Officer and several of her aristocratic local connections, he'd vocally and clumsily asked whether the coincidence in terminology might not be historically meaningful. Whether, perhaps, the soup had been initially made of, well, the intestines of other—things? Not fetal sheep? But, you know, fetal—other—things?

The Mental Health Officer had been unimpressed. Sticking to the salad, she'd suggested that Kurt explore his interest in the darker periods of the region's—her region's—culinary history in his upcoming series of sessions with her. After which, he'd been abashed. And rightly so. Because whereas in every other part of his life, Kurt was as smooth and muted and inoffensive as a Consul General ought to be, the moment he entered a kitchen—or a boat, upon leaving a kitchen—his exuberance got the better of him. He couldn't stop himself. He was inspired. He wanted to talk about these things to anyone who would listen. He relished his captive audiences.

Even so, in that one case, he ought to have remembered the identity of his interlocutor. The Mental Health Officer's peevish rectitude. Her almost religious faith in the redemptive qualities of civilized thought and behavior. In *not* inserting things into one's body that were never meant to be there.

Kurt paused in his recollections. Though, now that he was dwelling on the memory, he had been hearing some odd talk about the Mental Health Officer recently. Something about volatile solvents and a fish? He shook his head. The Consul General, to the extent that he could, tried

117

to ignore gossip that reached him from the lower reaches of the fortress. It was always malicious, and it was rarely accurate enough to be actionable. Or interesting.

He continued musing. The point was that although he might occasionally lose himself in an ethically complicated recipe, and although his attitude to the kitchen was perhaps not best suited to the Platonic ideal of a Consul General, he needed the cooking to keep himself sane. As a release. And anyone with eyes in his or her head to see would agree that he very much needed a release at the moment. Especially now. The past months had been more than beastly to him.

First, for example, there had been the apology and the bribe that he'd been forced to extend to the owner of that dance club that had thrown itself into the path of one of the Consulate's troop transport vehicles. Not to mention the loss of the vehicle itself, which was currently serving as the club's coatroom. Or, for that matter, its passengers, whose families back home continued to pester him about "updates on the search." He couldn't help the use of imaginary air quotes as he ruminated on the endlessly tiresome demands they made on him. He was no better positioned than they were to understand how a truckload of intoxicated young men could vanish into nothingness. And yet, they refused to leave him in peace.

Moreover, as far as Kurt was concerned, the owner of the club ought to have formally thanked his—Kurt's—nation for the publicity the accident had garnered his business. Worldwide. And the families of the transport truck's missing passengers ought to have apologized to the Consulate, as a collective, for sending it unstable soldiers.

But no, his Ambassador, a man with a tiny imagination in Kurt's opinion—though Kurt of course never voiced that opinion—disagreed. And so, there was Kurt on the Republic's state-run television station, groveling and apologizing for the "misunderstanding." Wasting his time looking "concerned" and "empathetic" during video chats with the grieving mothers. With an effort, he forced himself to relinquish the imaginary and skeptical punctuation. It wasn't doing his mood any good.

Then, tense, he continued thinking. Because, of course, there also remained the ongoing mystery of the disconcerting little rocks, some with rudimentary and, Kurt always thought, reproachful, facial features, that kept appearing in odd locations throughout the building. Evading security and leaving everyone jumpy. Clearly a prank, but when three had materialized on his windowsill, scrutinizing the crème brûlée he was idly caramelizing with a blowtorch to take his mind off an upcoming Exchange Program donors' celebration, he'd called in the Marines. The rocks simply weren't right. Predictive, he felt, of some future horror that his mind refused to shape into something coherent.

The Marines had shot them. With great vigor. A decisive and violent act that had provoked in Kurt a minute or two of giddy pleasure. Sadly, soon dissipated.

Thinking of the Marines, Kurt turned his morose reflections to the state of the monument out front—an art object that, granted, appealed to him not at all, as it always left him feeling faintly ashamed of his own country's effete and dainty founder in the face of the Republic's towering masculinity. Regardless of his feelings about it, however, the Marines were meant to protect it, and they were failing woefully in their duty. The thing was crawling with children at the moment. More and more every day. One could scarcely make out Our Great Founder's celebrated moustache under the layers of terrorist boy band t-shirts. Or his military boots. The small, undernourished bodies were everywhere, and no one quite knew how to respond to them.

Kurt himself felt especially aggrieved by the development, because in a moment of jovial intercultural exchange, he'd purchased a toothbrush from one of the scrappier and more charming of the boys. And after one use, the toothbrush had left him with a suppurating herpes sore on his lip. Providing him, it's true, with an excuse therefore to cancel the video conference with the mother of that student who had disappeared into the abandoned coffee shop. So, in the end, things had turned out fortunately.

But even the encouraging conclusion to the herpes-infested toothbrush incident left him irritable. His mask of solicitude, he knew very well, would have cracked had he been forced to keep that appointment. For surely they couldn't expect him to keep track of every overly curious student who wandered into the "foreign" quarter in search of caffeinated beverages? And really—who didn't know that the coffee shop was a death trap? It had been the student's own fault. Even the Mental Health Officer would have agreed with him there. Wherever she was at the moment.

Come to think of it, Kurt hadn't seen the Mental Health Officer for several weeks now. Since the evening she'd emailed him about that very coffee shop. And the street children? Something about a cultural infection introduced from the north... He closed his eyes, trying to call up the digital conversation—yes. And a party, and, possibly, opening an informal diplomatic channel to the underworld?

In fact, she'd been more agitated about it all than was her usual calm and self-controlled habit. But then, he'd assumed at the time she'd been writing metaphorically. Or, perhaps, medico-psychiatrically. The Mental Health Officer was a difficult person to parse on occasion—when necessary, he called in Commander of the Marines to translate—and Kurt found it best simply to agree with her and hope that she went away.

Well, she was away now. He tried not to feel too relieved about that. Then he curled up in his desk chair, cradled his forehead in his hands, and moaned.

Because the true problem—the one that capped the rest, that left the others negligible by comparison—had just shoved its way into his cerebral cortex. Which meant that now it was stuck there. He'd never rid himself of it. His daughter. Callie. The eternal headache.

Admittedly, she was mostly out of his sight these days, having taken up the internship with the Economic Affairs people. But even without being forced into daily contact with her, Kurt found it impossible to ignore the atmosphere she'd left behind. In the form, the constant form, of the boy.

The boy. He winced in the midst of his interior rant. Tried to curl into a tighter ball. He simply didn't know how to react to Callie's son. The boy's mere existence, his life, was a source of bewilderment to Kurt—and not in an intellectually interesting fetal-sheep-intestine-soup sort of way.

For his daughter, Callie, was a lesbian. She'd always been a lesbian. From the time she could walk or speak in complete sentences, it had been clear to all onlookers that she preferred the company of girls, and only of girls. Later, she'd liked women. And only women.

Kurt, for his part, had been delighted both by his daughter's preferences and by her certainties about those preferences. He'd dreaded, as he'd watched her developing in the early years, the increasing likelihood of a soul-searching psychic break preceding some agonized revelation of her "true" self when she reached adolescence. He metaphorically slapped his hand for sinking back into the snide use of imaginary quotation marks.

But he needn't have worried. Callie had been confident, and thus she'd been gratifyingly free of any need to transform her family into bit players in some theatrical display of narcissistic self-discovery. She was comfortable with her desires, and she acted upon them with a refreshing absence of performative angst. Quite simply, she enjoyed the company of women.

An open-minded and lazy person, Kurt was comfortable with her desires too. And really, his only wish, in general, was for his daughter's happiness (provided, of course, that her happiness didn't intrude itself too insistently upon his own pleasures). Meaning that when she'd joined that collective of radical feminist activists in the orbit of the chilly virgin who ran Visa Services, Kurt had applauded and encouraged her. And when she'd then gone on to involve herself in an exclusive relationship with the virgin, he'd been as supportive as it was possible for a father to be. He'd even forced himself not to dwell with excessive curiosity on what they all did with one another.

In short, his good wishes toward his daughter and her desires had been genuine, untainted, and true. He'd thought her well-raised and on an upward trajectory. He'd been proud.

Until, that is, she'd turned up pregnant. Four years ago. Ejected from the company of the virgin, shunned by the radicals who had once admired her, Callie had staggered into his office on the top floor of the fortress, weakly elephantine, and had vomited into his wastepaper basket. Still nauseated even in her thirty-ninth week of pregnancy. A taste of things to come, given the monstrosity that she was gestating.

But at the time, Kurt had felt nothing but concern. And, again, bafflement. He'd wanted to help. He'd also, despite himself and his belief in distant parenting, wanted an explanation. When the explanation had come, however, his initial reaction had been to withdraw the offer of help. Because the explanation, even channeled through Callie's unmistakable tearful distress, had been nonsense. Her story wasn't possible. Which meant that something even more sinister than what she was attempting to sell to him must have been the truth. And he'd been as grieved by her dishonesty as he had been by her despair.

According to Callie—Kurt continued to hold his head in his hands as he recalled the conversation—she'd had no intention of betraying the virgin who ran Visa Services. Certainly not with a man. And when she'd been propositioned by some stray male during one of her visits to the archaeological site where they'd been finding all of those ominous little rock sculptures, she'd laughed at him. Mocked his interest. Turned him— emphatically—down.

"Which man?" Kurt had asked.

124

"Some second or third cousin of Our Great Founder," Callie had replied ambiguously.

Kurt had thought for a moment. And then: "the one with the Olympic medals in table tennis?"

Though angered by the betrayal of his daughter, he might have been satisfied by that one as a father to his grandchild. The man's wrist movement was remarkable.

"No?" she'd said, still uncertain. Almost in the tone of a question.

"The one who makes socially conscious art out of pipe cleaners?" Less impressive, but Kurt had read an interesting article about him in the international edition of the state-run newspaper. Several factories had been given over to producing pipe cleaners solely for his work.

"No." Thinking slowly.

"Not the ice dancer?" Unless both had been equally confused.

"No." She wrinkled her forehead. "The angry one, I think. The one who leads the rebellions? Cutting down all that fencing wire they put up along the border when they're reeducating the peasants. You know the one, right? I think he shot paintballs at the Prime Minister once."

"Oh dear." Kurt had been troubled. The ice dancer would have made his job of smoothing things over infinitely less difficult. If mildly surreal.

But then, remembering Callie's words, Kurt had rallied. "You said you *think* it was the rebel. You're not certain."

"I can't be certain."

125

He'd paused again. More confused than ever.

"Callie," he'd finally said. "How can you not be certain? Look at yourself."

"He was in disguise."

"As what?"

"Camilla. In Visa Services."

At which point, Kurt had merely stared. Our Great Founder's male relatives conformed, without exception, to a single type: solid, hirsute, and muscular. Some were a bit taller. Some were a bit shorter. But all were thick, sturdy men with copious and opulent body hair. Even the ice dancer. He'd made it a part of his act.

Camilla, the virgin who ruled Visa Services, was pale and willowy. What little hair she had was cut into a spare, nearly transparent wedge that fell smooth and sharp from her scalp to her cheekbone. She'd spent a decade as a professional dancer before inaugurating her career in the diplomatic corps. Her signature role had been in *La Esmerelda.*

"But," Kurt had ventured, "how could he possibly have disguised himself as Camilla?"

"He wore a dress."

"Oh."

Kurt had seen the man a few times in grainy footage of the camps at the border, and he tried to imagine that body in one of Camilla's bias-cut silk tunics. The feather-light cashmere sweaters that she preferred. Though the image had brought a smile to his face, he'd remained flummoxed.

126

With a touch of regret, therefore, he'd set the picture to the side. If Callie wanted him to play along with her story, he was willing to do so. She was, after all, his daughter.

"All right," Kurt had continued. "So he wore a dress. And you mistook him for Camilla."

He'd forced down the smile. For her sake. She was still weepy, and there was a spot of vomit on her chin. She didn't deserve his amusement.

"What about as it, you know, was happening?" He'd stopped, choosing his words with care. "Surely his, uh, approach differed from what you'd experienced with Camilla?"

She'd extracted a package of facial tissue—a product of the street children outside—and wiped her eyes and nose. Kurt had winced, imagining the herpes, but he'd said nothing. Then, composed once more, she'd spoken.

"I thought she was trying something new." She'd crushed the tissue into a small, wet ball in her palm. "She did that sometimes. That's why I *liked* her."

And then, she'd broken down sobbing yet again.

Kurt had reached over and patted his daughter's shoulder. Still not quite believing that the situation—the current situation, that is; the back story she'd told was beyond fanciful—was real. But a glance at her distended belly had brought him back to the problem facing them.

"When did you realize you were pregnant, dear?" He'd wiped his hand, damp from the sweat of her hot, shuddering shoulder, on the knee of his trousers. "I mean, why are you only telling me now?"

"I thought I was just getting fat," she'd said. "And that's okay. Because different people have different body types. But then, yesterday afternoon, we all went swimming—you know, at that women's football club they opened near the end of the channel? And Camilla told me to leave." She was whimpering. "She said I'd betrayed her. She never wanted to see me again."

Callie had thrust her sodden face into Kurt's chest and moaned in despair. "So, I came here. What will I do? Whatever will I do?"

Kurt, despite his displeasure at the spot she'd been making on his dress shirt, had patted her shoulder again. "You're my girl, Callie. We'll take care of the child together. We've certainly got the resources. And if you'd like, I'll raise him as my own. You go back to Camilla. If you explain to her what happened," he'd added, unable to stem the babble escaping from his own lips now, "I'm certain that she'll understand. You just tell her exactly what happened. Like you've told me."

That had been his first mistake. Camilla, far from forgiving her erstwhile lover, had instead driven Callie mad. And the latter now staggered about the fortress like some punch drunk bear. Moaning and clumsy. Noticeably not herself.

His second mistake had been not leaving the thing that she bore—in her forty-third week, alone and seemingly cursed—exposed on a mountaintop. He'd had no idea that a child could be as vile as what Callie had pushed out of her uterus. Though its hair alone declared it, indubitably, to be of Our Great Founder's line. So, at least she hadn't been lying about that one detail of the story.

AND now, these interminable Exchange Program social events were not only keeping him from his cooking, but also keeping him from his ongoing plans to rid himself of the boy. Kurt had considered every possibility for achieving the latter, as the boy had inexorably aged and come into his vicious personality—including exchanging the brat for the grinning street child with the diseased toothbrushes. Denying any relationship if his true grandchild attempted to reclaim his position. Though Kurt doubted that he would. A boy like that would relish time spent in the underworld, spreading illness and addiction.

Switching him out for one of the swarming street children, however, was more a fantasy than a strategy. Kurt knew that, given the boy's impulses, the only effective solution would have to be a permanent one. The question that plagued him, therefore—and had plagued him now, for more than three long years—was how to undertake that solution without leaving evidence. The Consulate couldn't survive another scandal. A visit from the Republic's domestic police force.

He glanced out his office window at the backs of the Marines' heads. There were fewer of them these days, he believed, but then, he rarely counted or paid them a great deal of attention. Nicely decorative, of course, as a group. But hardly useful. And if their numbers were dwindling—that is, dwindling in such a way that the diminution presented the Consulate with a problem—he'd be certain to find out about it. Be informed.

Disgruntled, he lifted and examined a small and deadly screwdriver that he'd confiscated from the boy when he'd discovered the latter using it to remove the eyeball of an immobilized feral dog. All anyone ever brought to him were problems. With increasing frequency he found himself wishing that sometimes, occasionally, they'd *not* inform him. It wasn't as though the world would end if he were kept in the dark a few times.

He opened the top drawer of his desk and tossed the screwdriver inside. It landed hard, disturbing the heap of other items he'd confiscated from Callie's son. The packet of rat poison that the boy had attempted to pour into the vat of blueberry muffin batter they used in the food court. "Teaching them to bake," he'd called it, giggling and retreating into the labyrinth of the internal fire escapes. The basket he'd carefully woven from hair he'd surreptitiously cut from the heads of visiting dignitaries. "Teaching crafts." The many, many household items he'd used to kill the myriad small animals—sufficiently numerous that closing the drawer properly had become difficult. "Hunting." And then, of course, the tiny pistol,

filched from the shooting range, with which he'd
nearly killed his mother.

Kurt paused to remember the incident.
Shuddering and depressed. She'd frightened him,
the boy had explained later, during one of his
sessions with the always understanding Mental
Health Officer. He'd mistaken her for a bear.

A lie, of course. Though in this one case,
Kurt had wondered what Callie had been playing
at with the boy. Stumbling after him, her arms
wide, grunting her love. When she herself had
been questioned, she'd claimed that she'd wanted
nothing more than to demonstrate her affection for
him. But then, Callie's mind had already gone by
then. One more casualty of the grim judgment of
the virgin of Visa Services. Yet a third time, Kurt
shuddered.

Not that it mattered, of course. And in any
case, Callie had been easily neutralized a month or
two after the incident. Swept off to Economic
Affairs and forgotten. Unlike the boy. The terror.
Always underfoot. Throughout the Consulate.
Appearing even in Kurt's well-protected office,
bypassing the multiple cordons of military security
with such skill that Kurt had begun to wonder what
his nation was purchasing with its billions in
defense spending.

And the boy was, truly, underfoot. For, try
as he might to locate a nanny or a minder or a
teacher for his grandson, Kurt remained
perennially unsuccessful. The boy simply wouldn't
be watched. He certainly wouldn't be taught. On

the contrary, he metaphorically burned out the eyeballs of anyone who tried. And as much as Kurt's staff, acquaintances, and officers were frightened of him, the Consul General, they were exponentially more frightened of the boy. Kurt was their leader. But the boy was uncanny.

Thus, sneering, violent, and unappeasable, the child trailed Kurt throughout the Consulate. From his office on the top floor to the kitchen in the basement, a significant portion of which had been set aside for the Consul General's private use. From the founders sculpture outdoors to the dim, windowless interior cells that were the bailiwick of the Economic Affairs Liaison. Though if asked, Kurt couldn't be certain why she needed them. His staff had become used to ignoring the presence of the boy. At least when the boy wasn't assaulting them.

Kurt pushed back his desk chair and stood. He didn't know where his grandson was at the moment, and he didn't care. But he himself needed to lift his mood. And an hour or two spent in the kitchen would help with that. Buttoning his suitcoat, he left his office, nodding at the pretty Marine standing guard just outside.

He didn't have a great deal of time for culinary experimentation this afternoon because he'd been roped into an outing with three of the more prominent Exchange Program donors that evening. But to counterbalance the truncated time he had before him, he'd convinced them to meet him at the dock for a cruise on the *Oppenheimer*, rather than at some dreary hotel restaurant for a bland and endless meal. He paused for a moment in the corridor. Cogitating.

Kurt didn't ordinarily showcase his skills to people of donor status, but he might, perhaps, indulge in an exception tonight. For reasons of self-esteem, if nothing else. And perhaps they'd enjoy the fake intimacy that eating his own cooking would imply. Not, again, that he cared one way or the other. But it was a thought that supported his own inclinations, and so he clung to it.

When he reached the kitchen, luck remained with him. It was empty, as he preferred it. And on the other side of the wall that it shared with the shooting range, he could hear the Commander of the Marines practicing. Which encouraged him further. Kurt liked the Commander of the Marines. An undemanding person. And a perfect shot, from what Kurt understood. Talent of that sort was always helpful to the Consulate's public relations.

To the rhythmic, muffled sound of a weapon being discharged, Kurt thus began to assemble his materials. First he removed his suitcoat, hung it on a hook in a cupboard, and tied an apron over this shirt and trousers. Then, washing his hands, he began removing ingredients for the offal-stuffed pastries he planned to serve to the donors. A fussy recipe, but one that would occupy his mind. Force him to concentrate. Help him to forget his other—

133

A bottle of wine vinegar whipped past his head and smashed against the steel freezer behind him. Kurt tensed, turned, and stared at the liquid pooling onto the stone floor. But he knew already the source of the disturbance. His gorge rose.

"Ew." The boy trotted across the kitchen, pulled himself onto the counter that Kurt had prepared, and prodded at a calf's liver wrapped in paper. "Gross."

"It won't be gross once I've prepared it," Kurt replied, insincerely affable. "Wait till you see. It will be—"

The boy grabbed the wrapped meat and lobbed it after the bottle of wine vinegar. It landed with a wet splat in the puddle. "Gross."

Kurt forced his shocked features into an approximation of mild grandparental disapproval. Then, bending over to retrieve the liver, he spoke. "Now, now. We shouldn't treat our food in that way. It's impolite."

He returned the packet of meat to the counter and attempted to smile at the boy. The boy snatched it up and threw it against the freezer again. The paper split, and brownish liquid joined the vinegar on the stone floor.

"Why not?"

"Well," Kurt began, retrieving the liver once again, "because—"

The boy jerked it away and tossed it, discus-like, across the room. Kurt watched it land. And then he took up his meat cleaver and chopped off the boy's head.

It was only when the spouting blood had coated his dress shirt through the apron that he fully understood what he'd done. But when realization hit, his most coherent reaction was neither horror nor despair so much as a sort of sheepish embarrassment. Chagrin that this solution hadn't occurred to him months—years—before. He'd been so stupid.

If anyone was capable of dealing with the evidence the boy had left behind him on the block, Kurt was. The Consul General was in his element. Doing what he did best. He needn't even change his recipe all that dramatically.

And so, over the next two hours, Kurt concentrated on stuffing intricate puff pastries with carefully seasoned assortments of meat and offal. Twisting them into fanciful and attractive shapes. Placing them on trays in the oven. Leaving a few, uncooked and covered with plastic wrap, in the freezer for later.

When he'd finished, Kurt mopped up the spilt vinegar from the floor and wiped his food-coated hands on his apron. The only conundrum he faced now was what to do with the head. An ugly little thing, still wearing its expression of sneering hostility. But the kitchen was well-equipped with sacks and containers for dealing with food refuse, and after wrapping the head in fix or six layers of clinging plastic, Kurt rummaged about in a cupboard until he found a sturdy, zippered, and opaque waterproof sack—a sack seemingly made for the transport of one's depraved, dead grandson's head.

Pleased, he dropped the muffled head into the bag, secured the zipper, and took up the heated case of pastries with his other hand. Though he'd washed only the worst of the blood from his hair and his clothing, no one seeing him leaving the kitchen in his current state would think twice about it. Kurt frequently roamed the halls of the Consulate soaked in blood, and his staff all knew that the reasons for his appearance were culinary rather than criminal.

Nonetheless, he spent a half hour further, upstairs, showering and changing his suit before setting out for the *Oppenheimer*. The Exchange Program donors would be expecting cleanliness and hygiene. And Kurt certainly didn't want to put them off their appetizers.

KURT'S arrival at the dock presented him with a surprise. Though not an unpleasant one. As he approached the boat, he saw, first, that the three donors were waiting with subdued excitement in the cockpit. He'd expected that. In addition to those three, however, (and, of course, the crew, the skipper, and several security officers), Kurt could just make out in the dim light of the setting sun a thickset and hairy middle-aged man, dressed as a peasant, staring balefully at him from the bow of the boat.

Hardly a mystery. Kurt had spent hours poring over hundreds of grainy, blurry photos of the pig who had ruined his daughter. Who had inflicted his demonstrably deficient genetic material on his—Kurt's—family. And so, he recognized the figure immediately.

Smiling slightly, and pleased by his last-minute decision to pack sixty, rather than fifty, of the puff pastries into the food carrier, he took a few more steps in the direction of the *Oppenheimer*. Careful not to jostle his luggage. Moving with slow deliberation.

The donors, he was glad to note, were thrilled rather than disturbed to be voyaging in the company of a notorious rebel leader—hence their thrumming excitement from the cockpit. Kurt couldn't have organized a more successful dinner entertainment for them if he'd tried. Which, aside from the food, he hadn't. Entirely uninterested in whether they were amused or not.

But their tolerant attitude toward the unexpected fourth guest made it easier for him to remain buoyant and energetic as he climbed, with the assistance of the skipper, from the dock to the deck of the boat. Clutching a sack in each hand. Which the crew, used to the Consul General's boating accoutrements, knew better than to offer to carry—an additional quiet relief to Kurt, who planned to toss the boy's head over the side a few hours into the tour, once the light was gone and his guests were sufficiently intoxicated not to notice a small splash. He would have trusted the crew not to peek in the sack anyway. But it was best not to tempt fate.

137

After nodding greetings to the three donors and ignoring the figure in the bow, Kurt descended to the galley to prepare his feast. And as the *Oppenheimer* cast off and forced its way across the wake of a pair of nuclear submarines, he hummed a nursery rhyme while arranging the perfectly browned, aesthetically flawless little rounds of pastry on several china plates. Unable to resist, he popped one into his mouth as he worked. And then, surprised by the success of the recipe, he ate three more.

His guests, to his continuing gratification, consumed the rest. And indeed, by the time the gibbous, nearly full moon had risen in the black sky, and the *Oppenheimer* was returning home, no longer fighting the current, not a crumb of puff pastry remained. Kurt had even taken a separate plate to the antisocial figure on the foredeck, who, bristling, had pulled the food into his lap. Then, staring straight ahead, not deigning to notice Kurt, he'd shoved a fistful of the pastry into his mouth. Chewed. Swallowed.

Satisfied that the father of his grandson had eaten his appetizer, Kurt himself had turned back toward the cockpit to entertain his more talkative guests. Before he'd taken two or three steps, however, the man had grunted in his direction. Bemused, Kurt had faced him once again.

"Yes?"

"Where's Callie?" the man had grumbled in Kurt's own language.

"In good hands," Kurt had replied, haughty. "Among people who care for her."

The man had grunted a second time and returned his gaze to the water. After a few seconds, Kurt had made his way back to the three donors. Drunk and affable, they were praising the famous hospitality of the Republic and its second city. Predicting a significant uptick in students choosing both for their immersion in alternative cultural mores. Kurt's stomach had lurched at that. But otherwise, he'd considered the outing a success. All had gone infinitely more smoothly than he'd hoped.

In fact, the evening had been such a success that Kurt didn't realize until he was checking his email the next morning that he'd forgotten to toss the boy's head over the side. His euphoria at the success of his recipe, and the almost sensual pleasure he'd felt in watching the pig who had ruined his daughter eating the liver of his own monstrous son, had entirely erased the sack containing the severed head from his mind. It was likely still wedged into the small second sink in the galley. Awaiting his attention.

For thirty or forty seconds, sitting in his office chair, Kurt had tried to reassure himself that the crew would simply have placed the sack in the rubbish with the remainder of the food detritus. As they always did. They had no reason to open and examine the contents of the bag—their jobs were difficult enough without inspecting food waste as well.

But the first new item in his inbox killed his weak optimism. He squinted at it. From the Ambassador's personal account. The subject heading read, "PHONE ME NOW," and there was no message. Only an attached image.

Swallowing, Kurt opened the file. It was a photograph of Our Great Founder's disreputable cousin, the rebel leader. Back on the border already. He must have travelled all night. Reaching his stomping ground, in fact, or at least so it appeared, just in time to begin haranguing a new crowd of beleaguered farmers. As was his wont.

This particular demonstration, however, was unusual. For sharing the makeshift stage with the bandit was a sort of floppy, clownlike doll. Supported by two or three tall sticks. More than unusual. The rebel leader was known both locally and internationally for reacting with swift and often inventive violence toward anyone or anything that claimed a portion of his audience's attention. Including large, creepy dolls.

Kurt enlarged the photo and looked at it more closely. No. Not a doll. His grandson. The bandit had reconstructed the boy's body out of what looked to be woven hair. And then he'd sewn the severed head to the artificial neck of the effigy. The thing was floundering at the end of the sticks beneath a banner at which, in the photo, the bandit was gesticulating in a sort of charismatic rage.

Like many of the banners and signs produced for his movement, this one had been drafted with international consumption in mind.

As a result, its slogan had been reproduced both in the language of the Republic and in Kurt's native language. It read: "if this is what the wolves do to their own babies, what will they do to YOU? Cannibals OUT!"

Kurt closed the attachment. And then, sighing, he picked up his telephone and dialed the Ambassador's private number. After ten or fifteen minutes of letting the man rant at and threaten him, he interrupted. Gently. Playing the only card he had.

"But sir," he said, "aren't wolves a highly respected animal here? If you think about it, the banner is almost a compliment. To our nation, I mean. Given the cultural context, you know—"

The Ambassador hung up on him.

And Kurt, wistful—but certainly not regretting his quiet certainty that his daughter's malignant offspring would never, ever launch himself into the open again—gazed out the window. Appreciating the backs of the heads of the Marines. In the pale blue sky, above their tense formation, he could see the full moon. Cold and distant.

He dropped his eyes to his clasped hands. And then, he wrinkled his forehead. His skin was hairier than he remembered. Almost furry. Disentangling his fingers, he examined his palms. Hairier even than those of Our Great Founder's line. Was it possible, he wondered, that he'd picked up the condition via his close contact with the pig in the bow of the *Oppenheimer*?

141

Then he shook his head. Impossible. And silly. Hair was genetic, not contagious. The state of his hands—and wrists, he vaguely noticed—was a product of overwrought nerves. He simply needed to calm himself. A visit to the kitchen would help with that.

He rose from his chair, feeling stronger than he had in ages, and moved in the direction of the door. Wondering what was cooking. Because, though it was early in the day yet, he could definitely do with some meat.

When the Marine guarding the corridor fainted at the sight of him, Kurt shrugged. The boy was decorative. Fragile. But it didn't matter. And he, Kurt, would keep mum about the soldier's weakness. The Consul General wouldn't trade his pretty retinue for the world.

CATTLE

TIME to move house. Flynn couldn't stand it anymore. Having squatted for what felt an eternity in the cramped former Embassy of that upstart Republic with the hermaphroditic founder, he was due for a change. Anyone could see that.

Not that he hadn't been pleased at the time, when his uncle had foisted the art déco pile on him. It had served its purpose well for decades. But now, officially, it bored him. He couldn't bear it. He repeated. With slight variation.

Dead uncle, Flynn reminded himself, yawning. Dead for nearly as long as Flynn had been immured in this wretched building. And the women back home still weeping and dripping over the nonentity. Pointless display. Though it did help the plants to grow.

He brightened and wriggled his fingers at a pedestrian in the street below him who was staring, aghast, up at the fourteen-foot-high window in which he, Flynn, stood, wearing an open peacock blue dressing gown and nothing else. Then he absentmindedly scratched the inside of his thigh

143

with a big toe. The pedestrian flushed, dropped his eyes to the pavement, and walked on.

He would, it's true, miss the friends he'd made in the neighborhood that orbited his house— a neighborhood that had grown over the decades into a globally celebrated meeting place for the sort of merchant who would sell anything and the sort of customer who would buy it. One of the few spots on the planet where the underworld bled into the realm of respectability with nary a border nor a line to distinguish the two. Here, and only here, the worlds were one.

The ethical black hole thus generated had driven Our Great Founder mad back in the day. Flynn smiled at the memory. Yes, he'd miss his friends if he left the old place.

And not only the ones with the needles and the riding crops, the glue and the hidden cameras. Innocents like the dismayed man in the business suit, who still remained visible, scuttling away down a narrow alley beyond the edge of the building, were as precious to Flynn as any of his closer confidantes. Financial advisor to one of the bondage clubs, no doubt. A thought that brought further joy to Flynn's morning.

The Republic was an upstanding country in so many, delightful ways. People worked hard. Payed their taxes. Did their part to survive. He craned his neck until the figure had disappeared, and then he belted his dressing gown and turned away from the window.

His name wasn't actually Flynn. But he'd chosen the moniker upon taking possession of the building, and then he'd kept it throughout his residence there, because the letters had grown on him. The "f" and "l" at the beginning made his tongue feel nice when he pronounced them together. And making his tongue feel nice was an important part of Flynn's life. Whereas the double "n" at the end reminded him visually of a gated doorway. Nearly as pleasing as the feel of the "fl."

But, despite all of that, he knew that he'd be abandoning the place soon. He lowered himself onto a gold silk sofa, unbelted his dressing gown, and sipped from a tiny cup of perfect espresso that his boy had left for him. Inhaling the aroma.

He didn't have a chance to appreciate the aroma for long. Even before the caffeine had begun to play with his dopamine, a glum and tolling echo announced the arrival of a visitor. The sonorous vibration a holdover from the building's origins as an edifice meant to intimidate.

Flynn groaned and flung his head back on the armrest of the sofa. Smiled a brief good morning to the Oreads disporting themselves in mosaic form across his gilded ceiling. The arrogant bitch was on time. As she always was. His primary impetus toward abandoning the house, the city, and the Republic as a whole. He could simply no longer—what was the word?—cooperate?— negotiate?—collaborate?—with her. Even in her current, amusingly diminished, form. Doing so only made him feel dirty. It was, in fact, the only activity in his life that made him feel dirty.

Forty-five seconds later, she was entering his drawing room, led by the sedate boy—nude, because today was Wednesday (why not?)— wearing one of the badly tailored bureaucratic skirt suits that she incorrectly believed leant her an air of menacing anonymity. She was disconcerted by neither the nudity of the boy nor the state of Flynn's own dressing gown, cast open to reveal his more mature attributes. Nodding her thanks to the boy, she sat in a golden chair that matched the golden sofa, accepted her own tiny cup of espresso, and gazed, polite, across the room at Flynn.

"Nice sunglasses." He moved his arm behind his head to support his neck. Still enjoying his ceiling. Speaking, contemptuously, in the language of her homeland.

"Forgive me," she replied in the dialect of his little Principality, refusing to cede linguistic ground. "Shall I remove them?"

She began to set her espresso on a table to the side of the golden chair. Moved her other hand in the direction of the glasses. He snorted at the easy threat.

"No. I'll join you." Rolling onto his side, he fished a pair of pitch-black Armani shades from beneath the sofa, rearranged himself on his back, and slid them over his eyes. "Now we match."

"Hmm." She retrieved her cup and sipped at the espresso. A few moments passed in

146

antagonistic silence. They each continued to think and speak in the native tongue of the other.

"You're here on behalf of your master?" he finally asked. The caffeine he'd ingested had done nothing for his mood.

"He's not my master."

"Have nine years passed so quickly, then?" He frowned up at the ceiling in fake consternation. "I must have lost track of the time. Not enough to do around the place to keep me occupied." He waggled his eyebrows like a Marx Brother. "But you'll soon see to that, won't you, Elaine?"

"Yes, Highness. I certainly will."

He grinned. They all called him "Highness" here. And they all hated it. Because yes, granted, he was the undisputed nephew of the neighboring Princelet via his mother. But his father remained a mystery to one and all—his mother, upon being questioned in proper patriarchal fashion as to the author of her condition, having responded with the classic (and Flynn had always thought, stylish) response: "it was dark."

Elaine especially begrudged him the title. He lit a cigarette with a lighter shaped like a pistol and inhaled a glorious lungful of smoke. Perhaps the caffeine had done its job, after all. Things were looking up.

"What, then?" He blew a long stream of smoke up at the Oreads. Aiming at the nearest one's vulnerable bits.

"The Consul General," she said pompously, "requests your protection."

"For what?" Bored.

"His cattle." And then she paused. Uncharacteristically muddled. "That is, you know, he calls them 'cattle.' Just as he's always done." She used the local word for "cattle."

"Cattle," he repeated in the same language. "And what does he do with these 'cattle?'"

She set her empty espresso cup on the table beside her. Not gently. But nonetheless managing to keep her visible frustration mostly in check.

"What does anyone do with cattle, *Highness?*" She fixed him with what he was confident, behind the glasses, was an icy glare. Or hot glare? Some variation on a glare, at any rate. "He herds them. From here. To there. He's prepared to negotiate with you for safe passage. Protection from the—the undesirables."

Flynn flicked a lazy glance in the direction of the boy, who had returned to the room. Standing just inside the door. Waiting for an opportune moment to collect the empty espresso cups.

"What about it?" Flynn asked the boy. "Do you consider yourself an undesirable?"

The boy remained impassive, waiting for instructions regarding the cups. And Elaine, finally giving in to her irritation, leaned toward Flynn, who was still stretched out on the sofa, blowing dilatory smoke at the ceiling.

"Must we do this every time?" She drew in her breath. "*Highness?*" Then, regaining control of herself, she clasped her hands together on her knees. "*Every time* I'm called upon to shift a herd for that idiot?"

"If you want your safe passage, Elaine, then yes, we do." He sat upright and crushed out his cigarette in his empty cup. "I enjoy it. And you, after what has it been?—seven years?—more?—still fail to understand the meaning of 'penance.' Patience, darling."

"Cunt."

He tilted his head, considering. "Not really."

And then, softening because unlike Elaine, he was at heart a good-natured person, he threw her the charming smile that remained the gravitational center of the neighborhood that he still, despite himself, adored.

"Allow me my little games and influences," he said to her. Cute and cajoling.

When she didn't respond, he shrugged and continued. "Fine. It's true. I've got an in with the underworld. The street kids, to their eternal discredit, like me. And I like them. Cope with it, Elaine." He paused, enjoying the vernacular of her homeland's imprecise yet hawkish language. "And, for what it's worth, I'll see to it that your Consul's cattle are left alone. I'll even do it for free this time. To demonstrate my good faith."

She rubbed her eyes under her sunglasses with a thumb and a forefinger. "Shit."

"What?" His smile hadn't wavered.

"I can't deal with this."

149

"Deal with what."

Abruptly, she stood. "I'm delighted, *Highness*, that you find yourself so endlessly fascinating. And I'm certain that you've got something terribly clever and brilliant planned for tonight's switch. But I give you my word—" she stepped closer to him, seeming to grow larger— "if you fuck with me on this one, I'll skin you alive and hang what's left from a tree."

"I've no doubt that you will." His smile faded, and he sighed. "But you'll feel guilty about it afterward."

"The herd," she told him, ignoring his tone, "is arriving from the north at midnight. Once they've docked, we're moving them to the Consulate's boat, which will be flying Consular flags, for the remainder of the journey. To avoid jurisdictional difficulties. You've got two jobs: first, show up. And second, keep your little wraiths off of us."

She tossed a packet of something wrapped in brown paper on the table beside her empty cup. "Your payment. *Highness.*"

He rose from the sofa to escort her to the front door. Didn't trouble himself to open the package. "I'll be there."

"Good."

Then, as he was tying the belt of his dressing gown, he looked sidelong at her with the same hint of a smile. Palpable beneath the Armani sunglasses. "Silly of me. I forgot to ask. How's that

boy of yours? What was his name? Daphnis?
Larry—"

"He's flourishing," she snapped. "Thanks."

THE water was agitated, whipped up into
petulant whitecaps, when Flynn reached the empty
Oppenheimer at ten to midnight. He was wearing
a thick fisherman's sweater, a close-fitting cap, and
corduroy trousers. Looking charming, as always.
Elaine, who was already waiting, wore the same
ugly apparatchik suit she'd worn that morning.

As they stood side by side, awaiting the
arrival of the herd from the north, Flynn shoved
his hands into the pockets of his trousers. Faced
the wind and the spray, enjoying the feel of the
weather on his face. Imagining how attractive he'd
be were anyone other than Elaine observing him.
But no one was. Depressed, he slumped his
shoulders.

"When did he begin herding cattle?" he
finally asked her. Largely to pass the time. Already
bored because immobility and waiting weren't in
any way his métier.

"I don't know," she said. "He began before
I arrived."

"He does it for what? Humanitarian
reasons?"

Surprised into a reaction, she turned to face
him. Not speaking.

"Sorry," he mumbled. "Stupid question."

"They're here." She pointed to a boat
gliding silently in reverse, its motor cut, into place

behind the *Oppenheimer*. They'd move the cattle directly from the one to the other. Keep them from setting foot on Republican soil. Plausible deniability.

"Why do you do it, then?"

She glanced at him a second time, now with overt dislike. "Penance, Highness."

"Ah." His voice was dry. "I'd forgotten."

"Cunt."

"I believe this is my cue," he said.

Pulling himself up onto the deck of the *Oppenheimer*, he nodded toward the skipper—who looked both furtive and terrified—and opened the hatch over the boat's small forward hold. Just large enough for a modest herd of cattle. After that, he jumped from the stern of the *Oppenheimer* to the stern of the boat from the north, which was now rafted behind it. And he began to shift the cattle, calming their agitated lowing, from the one to the other.

When just under half had moved, however, he stopped the transfer. Rubbing his hands together, he peeked up over the gunwale to make certain that Elaine was as distracted as any sane person ought to be in the midst of a tedious task like herding. She was. And so, lowering himself quietly back into the hold, he began returning the cattle he'd taken off the boat from the north. Shutting and locking the original hatch once they were all in place. Shushing them gently as they sensed a disquieting change in plan.

152

Finally, he moved ten or eleven mid-sized rocks that had been used as ballast for the boat from the north to the lower hold of the *Oppenheimer* to ensure that the Consulate's craft was floating convincingly low in the water. Until, satisfied, he untied the boat from the north, pushed it back, and began maneuvering it, so Elaine thought, in the direction of its home port.

She needn't know its true destination. Flynn himself scarcely did. But he was well aware of what the Consul General, and by extension Elaine, did with their cattle. Everyone was—though no one spoke of it. This group, unlike those, would at least have a fighting chance. He, Flynn, would make sure of it.

As Flynn passed the cockpit of the *Oppenheimer*, he noticed the face of its skipper. No longer furtive and terrified so much as smug and gloating. The man couldn't have been more obviously aware of Flynn's deception if he'd been winking and whispering about it over a beer.

Irritated, Flynn reversed the throttle of the boat from the north and allowed the craft to bump quietly against the side of the *Oppenheimer*. Then he eyed the skipper. Cool. Threatening.

"What did you see?" he asked in the language of the Republic.

"Nothing, sir."

"And so," Flynn continued for him, "you'll say nothing. Correct?"

"Yes, sir."

"I'll make it worth your while."

153

"Yes, sir."

"You saw nothing."

"I saw nothing."

The man swallowed, the fear that was more habitual to his features replacing the expression of acquisitive glee that had briefly transformed them. Indicating a sculpted stone figure that had been left behind in the cockpit by the talkative boyfriend of the Consul General's missing daughter, he continued. "That rock saw more than I did."

Flynn nodded, pushed the boat from the north back in the direction of the deeper water, and gave the man a little wave of his fingers. "Good."

But having relinquished the cattle to a field congenial to them, Flynn remained dissatisfied by the loose end in the form of the *Oppenheimer*'s skipper. Familiar as he was with corruption and dishonesty—and under ordinary circumstances, applauding and appreciative of both—he had read the man, despite the petrified promise of discretion, as very much for sale. Likely on sale.

After abandoning the empty ship at one of the dockyards serving the Republic's thriving pipe cleaner and fencing wire industries, therefore, he decided to run a test. Before returning home for a much-deserved drink and cigarette. Perhaps a bit of recreational time spent with the Oreads on his ceiling.

And so, collecting a group of street children to accompany him to the *Oppenheimer*'s usual moorage, he wrapped himself in the trench coat

and fedora favored by Elaine's contacts beyond the
Consulate, and went into action. Embarrassed by
the predictability of the disguise, but knowing that
the limited imagination of the *Oppenheimer*'s
skipper would respond well to it. That, in fact,
Elaine herself tended toward the tired and obvious
on those rare occasions when she was forced into
the field.

The *Oppenheimer* was just returning to the
dock when Flynn and the children intercepted it.
And as a result, even before the crew had secured
it and arranged its fenders, the children, gamboling
and giggling on Flynn's orders, were swarming it.
Saturating it with their presence. Up and over the
lifelines, across the foredeck, leaping into the
cockpit. Alarming the crew, which scattered into
the night, but trapping the skipper, who cowered
behind the wheel, offering them coins and other
bribes to leave him in peace. Not to touch him.

Flynn, adopting the gait of an angry pimp,
followed in the children's wake. Pulled himself
with slow menace onto the deck and approached
the cringing skipper. Then, staring down at the
man, he removed a riding crop from an interior
pocket of his trench coat—hardly fatal, but all he
could find about himself on short notice (he hid
the sequined handle up his sleeve)—and slapped it
thoughtfully three or four times against his thigh.
Struggling not to break his cover by dissolving into
laughter.

But the skipper, his guilty conscience
already plaguing him, was sufficiently convinced by

155

the display to recoil before the movement of the crop. Whimpering, he asked what the trouble might be. Indicating an abject willingness to cooperate. Flynn let the moment linger for close to a minute. And then, still agonizingly slow, he spoke.

"Herself," he growled, "has told me that she's missing a shipment."

"Oh?" Close to inaudible.

"Yeah. A few hours ago. Her contacts on the other side claim it never arrived." He and the street children drew into a tighter circle around the man. "She sent me to meet you. Try to clear up the misunderstanding. Right?" He thought for a moment. "Innit?"

Flynn didn't know what sort of accent or dialect he was attempting to emulate in the local language, but he was enjoying himself. And, again, whatever it was, it appeared to be working. Covering his head with his arms, the skipper was now squatting beneath the wheel. Weeping.

"Yeah." Flynn repeated. Uncertain as to why. But the repetition felt right.

"It wasn't me," the man finally moaned.

"What wasn't you?"

"I did what I was told," he said. "It was the pretty one. He stole the herd. Threatened me with—with terrible things if I ratted on him. So I took the boat out empty. Piloted it in circles for a few hours and came back." He was crying in earnest now. "I didn't know what else to do. It was the pretty one. The one with the attitude—"

156

"You can stop right there," Flynn told him. He'd removed his coat and straightened to his ordinary height. Kept the fedora because he decided he liked it. "I may be pretty, but I certainly don't—" He thought for a second or two. "No. No, you're right. I've got an attitude also. Fair enough."

The man had squeaked and thrown himself back against the aft lifelines when Flynn had revealed himself. Now, blubbering more than crying, he was attempting to explain himself. "No! You don't understand! I—I was—"

"Doing what you were told," Flynn finished for him. "Yes, I did get that." Furrowing his brow, he raised the sequined crop over his head and slapped the skipper eight or nine times about the shoulders and stomach with it. "You are a very, very bad man. Very bad. A bad, bad man."

Then, pausing, he examined the crop, which had begun to sag slightly in the exertion. Its handle had also bent and was twisted at an odd angle. He shrugged and tossed it overboard.

"Please," the man begged. "Please understand my position."

"Oh, I understand your position," Flynn shot back at him. He retrieved the little stone figure from the children who had been tossing it among themselves with muted shrieks since the conversation had begun. Shoved it into the face of the skipper. "You said that this rock had seen more than you had. This. Rock."

The man moaned. His hands over his face, shielding it from the eerily humanoid statue.

157

"*Did* this rock see more than you?" He waggled the stone. "Did it?"

The man shook his head, his face still covered. Flynn nodded. Returned the stone to the largest of the children, who immediately wound up to lob it in the direction of the second largest.

"No," he affirmed. "It did not."

The man whimpered again, but he said nothing more.

"You, however, are not worth my time." Flynn beckoned to the children and turned to leave. "No one will believe you anyway. And I don't envy you the conversation you'll be having tomorrow morning with Herself."

He squinted at a thin sliver of orange that had emerged over what was now dead calm water to the east. Corrected his earlier statement. "This morning."

And then, gathering the children, he disembarked the boat. Shot a stern glance at a girl who was attempting to smuggle the rock away with her under her ragged cotton shirt. Smiling at him, she let it roll back into the cockpit. After which, shy, she ran up beside him to hold his hand.

THE children saw Elaine and dispersed into nothingness a half second before Flynn himself did. Which meant that when he met her in the long shadows of the dawn at the end of the dock, he was alone. Briefly, he wished he'd kept the crop. Not because he was frightened. But it

158

would have been entertaining to watch her refraining from commenting on or reacting to it.

She halted half a pace away from him and fixed him with her opaque stare. "I know it was you."

"What was me?"

"Where are my cattle?"

"What cattle?"

She grabbed his arm and turned him back in the direction of the *Oppenheimer*. "Let's ask the skipper."

"Good idea," he murmured, allowing her to maneuver him back down the dock.

When they climbed aboard and reached the cockpit, Elaine exhaled, irritated. Gathered up the two small stone figures that were settled side by side on a thin cushion. One with longish hair. The other wearing what almost looked like a Neolithic variation on a peaked sailor's cap. Muttering to herself, she slipped both into the unsightly leather briefcase she carried to match her unsightly polyester suit.

"Damnit, Adrian."

"Who?" Flynn replied. Polite.

"Adrian," she provided. "A new officer I had promoted into my section a few months ago. He's got an interesting brain. And I thought the intricate work would take his mind off of this—" She indicated the rocks in her briefcase with a vague wave of her hand. "But it's only gotten worse. He drops them everywhere. Creepy dross."

"Oh." Bored.

She secured her briefcase. And then she looked about the boat. "Where's my skipper?"

Flynn wrinkled his forehead. "I don't know. He was here a minute ago."

"You've killed him, haven't you?" Her voice was tired.

"Why would I do that?" He sat on the cushion recently occupied by the stones and looked up at her. "I'm politely ignoring the fact that you've neglected to use my rightful title throughout this conversation."

"Where," she repeated, "are my cattle, Highness?"

"Look, Elaine. I don't even know what a cow is."

"Bullshit."

"'Bullshit, Highness,'" he corrected her.

"Bullshit."

"But that's precisely it," he said, dropping his insistence on the title. "It's not *bull*shit at all, is it? It's something else. I don't know what it is. I don't want to know what it is. It's icky."

"Icky?" She sat down across from him.

He shrugged. "It stinks. You ought to do something else."

She removed her shades, careful to keep her eyes averted from his, turned her upper body toward the east, and stared into the rising sun. "I've still got two years left. Highness."

"I'll trade you," he offered.

"What?"

"I've got something better than cattle." He reached into his back trouser pocket and pulled out a sealed plastic baggy containing a very small chip. Held it out to her.

She replaced her sunglasses and took it from him. Held the baggy close to her face. "What is it?"

"Tortoise." When he saw her look of incomprehension, he elaborated. "Well, 'TORTOISE.' An acronym for something or other. Your people like acronyms, I thought."

"Huh."

"Play with it," he pressed her. "You'll get a kick out of it." Still enjoying her dialect.

She opened her briefcase and carefully secured the baggy with the chip inside. "Thanks, Flynn." And then, almost, she smiled. "Highness."

He stood and stretched. Feeling sleepy, despite the fact that he rarely if ever actually slept. "And lay off the cows, will you, Elaine?"

She nodded and turned back toward the sun. While Flynn, without another word, hopped from the *Oppenheimer* to the dock. It was a perfect morning, he decided, to go shopping. He'd seen a pair of golden bedroom slippers in a window that would match his new fedora beautifully. And he did need to replace the sequined crop that the ocean had swallowed. Perhaps purchase a spare as well...

He began to whistle as he turned onto the sea road that led to the disreputable part of town he'd made his own. Perhaps he'd stay for a few more years in the city after all. If nothing else, the thought of abandoning the Oreads on his ceiling made him feel guilty. Difficult, really, to imagine what they'd do without him.

DAFFODILS

FLIGHT 613 to Frankfurt. That was when Hedda had made her mistake. Before then, she'd been happy and unaware. Fulfilled. A bright and talkative flight attendant utterly unprepared for the encounter with the woman in seat 3A.

At first, Hedda had believed it was a joke. Spycraft in the business class cabin. And though she'd kept a straight face when the woman in 3A had instructed her to watch and report on the activities of the man in 5C, she'd been giggling by the time she'd reached the galley. Heedless of the consequences of gossiping about the daft cow with the remainder of the crew.

Moreover, when the admittedly quite attractive man in 5C had taken her aside and persuaded her to distract the woman in 3A—to chat with her as he did something or other personal in the lavatory—Hedda had readily agreed. Still giggling. Better than a joke. A game.

But whatever the man had done in the lavatory, it hadn't been playful. Though, granted, it also had been derailed before it had gone too far. The plane hadn't gone down. No one had died. And certainly no one had blamed Hedda for the near disaster—or even considered the possibility that she'd been involved. The man in 5C had disappeared by the time the police had boarded. Which, as the horror had unrolled, had left Hedda shaking with relief.

But the woman in 3A had known. And, as Hedda had quickly discovered, she'd remembered. In brisk succession, Hedda had lost her job, her contacts, her friends, and then—in a single paralyzing, agonizing moment—her citizenship. Her identity.

Not officially, of course. There'd been no ceremony, no legal or political procedure. Rather, one day, dragging herself through passport control in the airport of a Republic she scarcely remembered, the sort she'd once enjoyed, just at the edge of touristic respectability, wondering yet again how she'd support herself now that her only skill was no longer marketable, Hedda had been met by a blank, bureaucratic wall. Her passport was invalid. All of her papers were invalid. She wasn't the person she claimed to be.

Neither a joke nor a game. And suddenly, with a single stroke of a keyboard, having been herded into a squalid little waiting area surrounded by plastic crowd-control barriers, she'd found herself unable to move forward. Or backward.

Entirely unable to make herself heard. Or understood. Until, washing up on the steps of the suburban Consulate that was her last, unlikely hope, she'd encountered the man from 5C. Less attractive than Hedda had remembered him to be. In every way less apologetic than he ought to be. But he had offered her a lifeline.

Taking her arm and walking her past a quivering heap of street children covering what may once have been some sort of art object, pulling her into a dismal food court lit by chilling LEDs, he'd sat her in an unstable chair and explained her situation to her. There was nothing that he could do about the steps that the woman in 3A had taken. She, Hedda, was stateless and voiceless. But he could see to it that she didn't starve. Hedda had considered the merits of starvation for a moment or two. And then, she'd nodded.

After that, the man from 5C had led her into the bowels of the building, saying something about "Economic Affairs." Placed her in front of a monitor. Introduced her to an unhappy apparatchik wearing sunglasses despite the twilit gloom of the field of cubicles that glimmered in the flickering screens. And then he'd left. She'd never seen him again.

HEDDA was an analyst. Her job was to observe the digital activity of local radicals and intellectuals and to flag any who appeared open to approaches from her government. "Her government." She tried not to dwell on the irony of the term because whenever she did, she teared up. Promising targets were sent along the pipeline until the best reached the desk of the Economic Affairs Liaison, who would then develop strategies of seduction.

A quirk of the software that she and the other analysts who inhabited the field of cubicles used—"TURTLE" or "LYRE," some acronym or other—was that its users were prevented from initiating contact. To block savvy targets from tracing conversations back to the Consulate, analysts could only reconfigure words and phrases already in play. They couldn't introduce new or original speech. Their tactics were heavily embedded in repetition.

Hedda found the work both tedious and pointless. Tedious because the majority of their targets wanted to be seduced, which meant that the secrecy and the intricately planned approaches, the covert cloak and dagger mystery of it all was pure theatre. Or, more accurately, pure masturbation.

Not only didn't it matter what the analysts repeated to their interlocutors, it didn't matter whether their repetition entirely changed the meaning of the digital conversation they'd joined. Hedda could have returned meaningless, moaning babble to her targets, and they still would have fallen happily to the Economic Affairs Liaison (or, so Hedda occasionally heard, the Economic Affairs Liaison working in tandem with the

Commander of the Marines). Their temptation was a foregone conclusion.

And pointless because, as far as Hedda could tell, once the Economic Affairs Liaison had added this or that target to her stable of informers, she never did anything with them. Her interest— and she frequently came close to stating so explicitly—was purely in the conquest. After they'd rolled over for her, they may have been animals or rocks or trees or weather conditions for all the attention she paid to them. Oddly, and notwithstanding her bitterness at her fate, Hedda felt a touch of spleen at the shoddy treatment of the fallen targets once they'd succumbed.

Thus (and also, of course, because she hated her job), Hedda frequently sought out inappropriate marks. Deliberately identifying the impossible ones. Intellectuals too neurotic to fall even for the Economic Affairs Liaison's wiles. Radicals whose purity of belief excelled their vanity or their venality. There weren't many of them. But they did exist. And Hedda, in the endless time she'd spent in the bowels of the fortress, staring at the flickering screens, had racked up an impressive collection of them.

If the Economic Affairs Liaison was displeased by Hedda's deliberate failures, she never said anything. And in any case, what would they do to her should she anger them? Send her home?

Hedda pushed back her lank hair and squinted at the green and black text scrolling in front of her. The target with whom she was dallying these days was a doozy. Educated variously in Paris, Leiden, and Los Angeles, he'd returned home to found eight different quasi-military pressure groups that ran the gamut of the left-right spectrum. Hedda couldn't tell whether he was confused or simply open minded.

She had, however, established that he was incorruptible. The flotsam she'd collected from the digital ether had made clear within the first hour or two of her investigation that the man had been approached by at least three governments aside from her own. "Her own." She bit her lip.

All three, however, had been quickly and roundly spurned. He'd derided their attention. Mocked them and, from what Hedda had seen, left them reeling. She herself, she'd thus determined upon piecing together the narratives of rejection, would be more circumspect. Not that she expected play from him even then.

Reading a few chatroom posts, she tried to get a feel for his interests. Anything that would entice his attention away from his single-minded pursuit of—well—whatever his ideological commitments were. The latter remained opaque to Hedda, which, though unusual, wouldn't have posed a problem under ordinary circumstances, had he been flaunting his radicalism in other ways. She'd encountered free-floating, contentless indignation before, and it was almost always nothing more than a fig-leaf covering for pure ego. Intellectual lingerie.

Her man, however, seemed as free of vanity—the usual complement to deeply held and deeply contradictory political beliefs—as he was of ideological coherence. Had he simply never examined himself, she wondered. Considered his reflection in a mirror? She'd rarely read posts or comments that were so passionately innocent.

Carefully, she followed the trail from the chatroom. A comment on a blog. Eight minutes of FaceTime with his mother that she watched, idly curious. Introducing a little virus into his mother's laptop as she left, because bitterness and disappointment do that to a person. Then she perused his shopping. Toothpaste, three pairs of socks, and a book of poetry. Emily Dickinson. For a few seconds, Hedda tried to derive political meaning from the choice. And then, admitting defeat, she let it go.

Frustrated now, she left her cubicle, wandered to the squalid corner of the field where a coffeepot eternally bubbled, and poured herself a paper cup of something vile and caffeinated. Then, rolling back her shoulders, she returned to her screen. And grinned. A flame war. Her man had stumbled into a toxic discussion board devoted to rare-earth metal extraction in the Republic's agricultural borderlands. Undertaken by her own nation, no less. "Her own nation." Settling into her seat, she sipped her coffee and prepared to be entertained.

She was entertained. But, despite her callous enjoyment of her target's increasingly hopeless case, she also found herself feeling troubled. Though lost and floundering, her man retained, unlike any other mark she'd previously seen in these situations, a certain dignity. The same innocence that had struck her earlier. And for the first time since the man in 5A had consigned her to the fortress, she felt a mild attraction to another person. A desire to help him, even if just a whispering bit, to free himself from the morass into which he'd fallen.

Scrolling through the ever more overwrought verbiage, unable to wipe the smirk off her face even as she chose her side, Hedda considered her options. There was nothing inappropriate about intervening. Intervention was her job. And should she actually manage to seduce the man, she'd earn nothing but praise from her colleagues. The fact that, just this once, her desires and those of the Economic Affairs Liaison coincided was a positive development. Not a situation that ought to disturb her. Or so Hedda silently told herself. All the while remaining very much disturbed, indeed.

She re-read two or three of the longer installments of the still-mushrooming toxicity. Identified a handful that looked likely. Scratched her cheek, counted to four, and then entered.

"...can possibly believe the propagandists and the politicians? There must be others out there who agree with me! Is there anybody out there? Anyone at all?" he had written.

Keeping to the software protocols, Hedda typed "anyone at all!" and hit "reply."

Waited twenty seconds. Ignoring her accelerated heartrate when the response came.

"Thank God. I thought I was alone. What's your background? Political philosophy? Activism? Grassroots work?"

Simple. "Political philosophy, activism, grassroots work." Reply.

"I thought so," he typed almost immediately. "I could tell. You're smart. Can you PM me?"

"PM me," she typed.

"I haven't got a handle or an address for you," he wrote. "I'm looking, but it's not here. A glitch, I think. Tell me."

Shit. "Tell me." Anything to keep the conversation going. She tapped her fingertips on the edge of her keyboard.

The response was slower this time. But, thirty seconds later, it came. "There's nothing to tell. My information is there on the screen. Where's yours? Upper right corner?"

She stared at the words for close to a minute. And then, taking a chance, she outed herself. Typing, "on the screen, upper right corner," she embedded an image. Inclusive of her location, should anyone trouble to look, because no one could completely sterilize an image.

A minute passed. Two minutes. Three. She cracked her knuckles. He'd troubled to look. And he'd not liked what he'd seen. Which ought to have been an obvious result to her. Her move had been more than stupid. It had been amateurish. Provoked by all of the wrong motivations.

She sighed and made a move to switch off her monitor. But then, to her quickly punctured joy, the response came. Lots of caps. Livid punctuation. Worse than she'd imagined.

"You fascist bitch. How dare you? HOW DARE YOU? You think I want anything to do with you or your government? NEVER, EVER, EVER FUCK WITH ME AGAIN!!!"

Hedda gazed at the text with hollow anguish. Feeling more gutted now than she'd felt stupid before. What had she been thinking? Something had been wrong with her mind. Sleep deprivation. Insufficient caffeine. Something. Her already thin sense of self was now stretched into something beyond tenuous. Tiny threads of nothing about to break apart entirely.

Her duty was to forget that she'd ever encountered him. Move on. She had a more than sufficient list of potential marks to absorb her attention. An endless list. Silently, calmly, she counted to ten. Fifteen. One hundred. The man remained stubbornly embedded in her thoughts. She began to cry.

And so, because the keyboard was there in front of her, and because she couldn't bring herself to give him up without a fight, she tried one final approach. In cringing, lowercase letters, she typed: "fuck with me again?"

Hoping. Stupidly.

There was no reply. She dropped her forehead into her hands.

THE Economic Affairs Liaison found her seven hours later in the same position. During her—the Liaison's—midnight sweep of the field of cubicles. Looking for snakes, she always said, though no one knew whether she was speaking metaphorically or literally.

Leaning over Hedda's chair and gazing at the screen, her sunglasses reflecting the green text, the Liaison skimmed the exchange. Then she pursed her lips. Stood.

"Not going well, huh?"

Hedda shook her head. Her forehead still in her hands.

"Have you experimented with the new add-on yet? Techs are calling it 'NARK.' Something about the numbing effect." The Liaison dug a flash drive out of her pocket. "Your man there would be an ideal lab rat. Might be a good time to try it."

Hedda looked up at her, dull eyed. "Try it?"

"Sure." The Liaison bent over and inserted the drive into Hedda's computer. "It's a great improvement over the original. Analysts needn't intervene personally at all. The software leads the target into a virtual chamber where all he experiences are his own words reconfigured and spit back at him."

"Spit back at him?"

"Yes. And who doesn't love the sound of his own voice? They can't get enough of it." The Liaison turned and began walking down the dim and drafty corridor of cubicles. "After that, they come to us on their own. Numb and spinning. Begging for more."

"More."

"Hmm." And she was gone.

Hedda's experiences with the woman in 3A and the man in 5C had left her with little in the way of empathy. And though she'd certainly felt an attraction to her target—a wistful sort of nostalgia for the purity of his innocence—she was also resentful. Increasingly resentful, in fact, with every passing minute.

He'd rejected her. He'd rejected everyone. Time, she decided, that he look in a mirror. Witness for himself the mayhem he'd caused with his constant, careless self-exposure. Erupting discussion boards would be the least of his problems.

Preparing for battle, she tied her hair back into a tight knot on the top of her head. Consumed the dregs of her cold coffee in three grimacing swallows. Returned to the original chatroom, watched for three minutes, and was in. Executing the program, she sat back and viewed it doing its work.

"...unfathomable cruelty inflicted on the people of the region," he had written. "It's..."

"It's unfathomable the cruelty the people inflicted on the region," her software replied.

"Precisely! And it's our responsibility to see how those contributing to the horror will be held accountable."

"Contributing to the responsibility," the software told him, "is precisely the horror those will see. How accountable!"

"You don't get more right than that!"

"Get that?"

"Yes! Yes, I do. It's been so long since I've spoken to anyone who understands what's at stake. Have you seen the workers and the soldiers out there? Are you there now? What do you think about..."

Hedda chuckled as her target became ever more enamored by and enmeshed in his own language. Falling deeper and deeper into the abyss. First annoyed by—and then blind to—any attempts from the outside to penetrate the chamber he was building up around himself. He saw no one else. He heard no one else. And, as the Economic Affairs Liaison had said, the moment she cut his connection to the software, he'd sink into withdrawal. Feel the need for the words so intensely that he'd do anything—*anything*—for a fix. For a continuation of the conversation with the brilliant, insightful man he'd glimpsed in the mirror. She was looking forward to that moment.

That is, she was looking forward to it for an hour or two. A few days later, as his narcotic linguistic spinning became both languid and frenetic, she began to feel guilty instead. The man was verbally wasting away. She was witnessing, in

175

real time, the disintegration of a mind—the demolition of a person, and his replacement by an accretion of ever more disjointed messages reconfigured and discharged back at him. Yes, he'd been incoherent and self-contradictory before. Now, though, he was splitting into pieces. She couldn't watch it.

Nor, she decided, did she have to. The man was gone. Beyond help. But that didn't mean he had to fall to her department—that she was consigned simply to watch and wait for the inevitable conclusion. Joining their stable. Forgotten. Better total erasure than that.

And so, with a furtive glance in the direction of the shadowy entrance to the cubicle field—reassuring herself that the Economic Affairs Liaison wasn't watching (though, of course, she was always watching)—Hedda ripped the flash drive from her computer. Dropped it into her coffee cup. And stared at the screen.

At first nothing. And then, with an explosion of pain that Hedda herself came close to feeling, a series of emojis flared up in a non-verbal scream of despair. Looking, if she tilted her head properly, a bit like a flower. After which, there was babble. Utterly meaningless babble. She observed it for a little over two minutes, wondering whether it would resolve into something coherent. But it never did. On and on and on, dwindling into fields of pretty nothingness. After fifteen minutes, she shrugged and turned off her monitor.

176

Obviously, she thought to herself as she collected her empty paper coffee cup with the flash drive inside, it was a shame for the man. All of that education, those good intentions, the passion and the certainty, and he'd ended as nothing more than a blot of digital effluvium. The verbal and intellectual equivalent of a passing, only half-perceived scent of a spring flower.

But really, in the broader scheme of things, it wasn't all that bad. She herself had been a keening ghostly voice, and nothing more than a keening ghostly voice, since her fuckup on Flight 613 to Frankfurt. And she was fine. We all make mistakes. Though at least hers, she reminded herself smugly, had been in the flesh. Wasting away in an internet chatroom was just plain pitiful.

HOUNDS

SHE's a virgin."

"Why does that matter?" Eyal was nervously buttoning his suit coat. Wiping his sweaty palms on his sleeves.

"I don't know." His brother helped him to straighten his tie. "But they told me you're supposed to keep it in mind. Or, you know, don't forget."

"That's weird."

"The whole thing is weird, Eyal." His brother held him at arm's length and examined the effect. "Are you certain you don't want me to go instead?"

"No. They sent the letter to me." He patted the pocket of his suit where he'd secured it. "It's my responsibility."

His nightmare. If he wrecked their chance, his brother would never forgive him. And why the Consulate had sent the interview invitation to him rather than to his clever and successful older brother was a mystery to them both. A bureaucratic accident, no doubt. One further baffling twist in their blind, three-year sprint toward freedom. Toward visas.

Eyal slipped his hand into the inside pocket of his suit to reassure himself that the invitation, his identification, and the copy of his application remained secure. Then he hugged his brother. And then, finally, he left the house. Walked up to the ridge road to await the bus that would transport him to the suburb and the Consulate.

It took Eyal two hours to clear the crowd-control barriers and security once the bus had deposited him at the foot of the fortress. Not that there was a crowd. Instead, a small trickle of people, mostly alone, but occasionally in twos or threes, trudged its way through the gates and turnstiles. As though queuing up for a carnival ride.

But each was vetted with care, each was asked to present his or her papers, and each watched as those papers were scrutinized with cold precision. Movement forward was the exception rather than the rule. For most of the two hours, Eyal simply stood immobile and practiced his interview technique. Occasionally he kicked aside a stray dog. There were several prowling the area. Though most were better fed than he'd seen elsewhere in the city.

When he reached the first set of gates, his papers raised no suspicions, and he was waved into a waiting area. Large. Dingy. Low-ceilinged. Cautious, he approached one of the plastic seats arranged against the walls, sat, and stared at his shoes. None of the eight or nine other people in the room attempted to make eye contact.

Forty-five minutes later, a pale, blank-eyed woman emerged from behind a closed door—one of many arrayed throughout the room—and, reading from a clipboard, announced his name. Smoothing the wrinkles from his suit, Eyal stood. Polite and diffident. When the woman beckoned to him, he followed her into a small, windowless office containing a desk, three chairs, and a decrepit computer.

The woman sat behind the desk and indicated that he ought to sit across from her. She extended her hand. After a brief moment of confusion, Eyal fumbled about in his suit pocket for his papers. Presented them to her.

Without altering her facial expression, the woman read through every page of the packet he'd given her. Then she turned to her computer, typed a quick note, opened a desk drawer, and extracted a sheaf of small cards held together with a blue rubber band. She removed the top card and pushed it across the desk at Eyal. Still cautious, he took it.

"That's your temporary card," she told him. "You'll bring it with you when you return tomorrow."

"Tomorrow?"

"Yes. Return to this level. You'll present the card and your papers to the assistant registrar's secretary." She switched off her monitor. "After that, your case will be seen by the registrar's committee."

"I understa—" Eyal jumped. Shocked.

"What is it?" The woman turned to look behind her.

"I'm sorry," he said. He was squinting into a dim corner of the room, to the side of her desk. "I thought I saw a dog."

"There's no dog here." Her voice was cool. Precise.

"No," he replied quickly. "Of course not. I'm sorry," he repeated.

"Take care not to lose your card," she said.

"Yes." He retrieved his papers, slipped the card into the envelope in which he kept his identification, and stuffed the packet in its entirety into his suit pocket. "Thank you."

"Good day."

T OMORROW?" His brother was sitting across from Eyal at their small dining table. Drinking beer from a bottle. Irritated.

Eyal, who had removed his suit jacket but was still wearing his cotton shirt—soaked through now with sweat—and his dress trousers, opened a second bottle. Eyed the jacket, which was hanging over an empty chair. The card and the papers were inside. He couldn't forget where they were.

"Tomorrow?" his brother repeated.

Eyal nodded. "She said I was to present my papers to the assistant registrar's secretary."

"The assistant what?"

"I don't know." Eyal emptied the bottle. "The place is cold. Weird," he added, echoing his thoughts from the day before. "She gave me a card."

"The Virgin?" His brother had perked up. "Was it the Virgin? That might explain the instructions."

"No." Eyal stopped himself. "That is, I don't think so." He considered what he remembered of the woman. "Well, maybe. It didn't come up. But I don't think she was, you know, *the* Virgin. The one they told you about. A virgin, maybe."

"Oh." Disappointed.

"So, I'll go back tomorrow. It's fine. We're moving forward." He rubbed his eyes. "If I play by the rules, it will work out." He knew that his voice was unconvincing.

His brother eyed his sweat-stained shirt and the lank jacket hanging over the third chair. "You've only got the one suit."

"I'll hang it up properly before bed. It will serve." Eyal pushed back his chair. "I'm going to sleep. Standing in that queue was deadly."

His brother nodded and nursed his beer.

The next day, Eyal spent close to three hours threading his way through the crowd-control barriers. And there were many more dogs in evidence than there had been the day before. Or, at least, Eyal was more attuned to them. Large dogs. Healthy dogs. Dogs that eyed him with

182

something other than passing curiosity. He kept his eyes on his dusty shoes.

When he reached the waiting room, however, he was called almost immediately. Pleased, he jumped up from his seat. And then he hesitated, surprised. It was the same woman. Casting her eyes lifelessly from empty plastic chair to empty plastic chair. Bored.

The same pale, listless face. The same nondescript beige or grey or cream suit. When he failed to move in her direction, she beckoned to him, curt, and retreated into her office. The same office.

Coming to himself, Eyal trotted after her. Bemused, he sat in the seat he'd occupied the day before and watched as she attended to her computer. When she extended her hand, he passed her his papers. The card she'd given him yesterday on top.

But before she could type the same note into her computer, he decided to assert himself. Confirm that he wasn't today sitting in her office in error. Though he would never claim to know bureaucracies as his brother did, Eyal was aware that loops of this sort did happen in large ones. Stories from his brother's visiting friends.

Clearing his throat, he spoke. "Am I not," he asked as politely as he could, "presenting my card to the assistant registrar's secretary today?"

"Yes," she confirmed as she typed, "you are."

Having completed her note, she opened the same desk drawer she'd opened yesterday and extracted a sheaf of cards held together with a yellow rubber band. Retrieving the card she'd given Eyal yesterday and replacing it with one that looked exactly the same, she pushed his papers across the desktop in his direction.

"That's your temporary card," she said. "You'll bring it with you when you return tomorrow."

"Tomorrow?"

"Yes. Return to this level. You'll present the card and your papers to the secretary to the registrar's committee." She stood, indicating that his appointment had concluded.

Eyal, still in his seat, came close to protesting—even if under his breath. But before he could form the words, he vaulted to his feet. With a small, involuntary shout.

"What is it?" The woman turned to look behind her.

"A dog," he said. "More than one. Back there." He pointed into the same dim corner into which he'd pointed the day before. "They're huge."

"There's no dog here."

"There is," he insisted. Still pointing. His hand shaking. "It's right over there."

But it wasn't. He could see plainly now that there was nothing in the room aside from himself and the woman. At least, nothing living. All that occupied the darkened corners of the office were unusually large and fluttering cobwebs. The space must be less well-used than Eyal had initially believed it to be.

"Take care not to lose your card," she said.

"Right." He patted the pocket of his jacket. "See you tomorrow."

"No," she corrected him. "Tomorrow your papers will be seen by the secretary to the registrar's committee."

"Whatever," he mumbled in his own language. Hoping as he turned to leave that she'd understood.

WHAT do you mean tomorrow?" His brother was sitting across from Eyal at the dining table again. The same beer. The same frustration. The same unyielding sense of impotence.

"I'm to go back tomorrow," Eyal said. "They want me to bring a different card."

"Did you bring the wrong card this time?"

"No." He took a swig of his own beer. "They switched that card for another. Apparently I'm making progress."

"Look, Eyal. Let me come with you. Something isn't right."

Eyal shook his head. Thinking of the gates, the fences, the security checks, and the crowd-control barriers. "They wouldn't let you in. And then I'd have to begin all over again." He ran a fingertip down the sweating neck of the bottle. "If they let me."

"It's not right."

185

"There's something else," Eyal said, looking up at his brother.

"What?"

"They've got these dogs. Everywhere. Spooky dogs." Eyal shivered at the memory. "I don't understand it."

"Police dogs," his brother asserted.

"I don't think so."

"To sniff for drugs."

Eyal shook his head.

"Bombs."

"No." Eyal rubbed his cheek. "They're more like strays. Wandering about in the queue. Sneaking into the offices. Watching the applicants. The woman claims she can't see them."

His brother stared at him. And then he reached across the table and slapped the top of Eyal's head with the palm of his hand. "Idiot. You've lived your whole life in this city. Twenty-three years. You've never seen a stray dog? And rather than concentrating on what needs to be done, you're watching the fucking dogs? Pestering the fucking Virgin about them? God help us."

"They aren't normal dogs."

"What are they? Police dogs or strays?" His brother had crossed his arms, stubborn.

"I think they're more like hunting dogs," Eyal said slowly.

"What do you know about hunting dogs?"

"Nothing," Eyal admitted.

"Idiot."

"I'm going to sleep." Eyal stood. "And I want to try to air out the suit."

The next day, Eyal spent three and a half hours waiting behind the crowd-control barriers. Perspiring in the open air. Nervously side-stepping the dogs, which felt now as though they were circling for a kill. Swarming.

But when he glanced surreptitiously at the other visa applicants scattered throughout the queue and then, nearly four hours later, in the waiting room, they were untroubled by the canine presence. Perhaps, as his brother had hinted, they were focusing on more important things. Eyal himself could scarcely remember to move when he was told to move, so unnerving was the pack that tracked him everywhere. But then, unlike his brother, he wasn't a businessman.

At least, he told himself wanly, the dogs kept his mind off of his irritation when the same insipid woman holding the same clipboard stepped out of the same dusty office to call his name. Otherwise, he might have made a scene. Said something unwise to her. But he didn't. The dogs intimidated him. Patting at the now near-permanent wrinkles of his suit, he merely stood, cowed, and followed.

Today playing the secretary to the registrar's committee, the woman indicated to Eyal that he ought to sit in the same chair. Typing a note on the same computer, she then switched the card he'd brought to her with an identical card from a stack held together with a black rubber

band and ordered him to return the following day.
Only the mastiff growling at him, stiff-legged in the
doorway, prevented Eyal from snapping something
rude at the woman that he and his brother would
both regret.

As it was, however, Eyal simply froze,
stared, and made a quiet and involuntary wheezing
noise upon taking stock of the door. The woman,
a step or two behind him, holding the clipboard in
preparation for her next applicant, cleared her
throat. Signaling to him that he ought to move.

When he didn't move, she stepped
delicately around him and through the door. And
in the split second that Eyal had managed to turn
his head to watch her progress, the dog had
disappeared. Twisting back, Eyal saw that the door
was clear. Empty. Aside from the woman, who was
returning now, followed by a jittery man wearing a
suit identical to Eyal's own.

Eyal edged around the pair and stepped
into the waiting room. Where he stumbled to a
halt. Nine dogs. Stretched out under the plastic
chairs. Languid. Many with their tongues lolling
out of their mouths. But nonetheless alert.
Watching him. And—a quick glance about the
space confirmed—him alone. The few other
occupants of the room may not have been there
for all the attention the dogs paid them.

Shuddering, Eyal strode in the direction of
the exit. Making no eye contact. With human or
with canine. Vowing that tomorrow, he'd progress.
Tomorrow he'd make a move. Take control of his

fate. Perhaps his brother might advise him. His clever and successful older brother always knew how to remove or—more often—elude the sort of obstacles that had always baffled and thwarted Eyal.

YOU'VE got to do something." His brother was sitting across from Eyal at the dining table.

"Yes," Eyal agreed. "But what?"

"Find another contact. Another clerk." His brother opened a bottle of beer and placed it in front of Eyal. "The one you've got isn't working. She's got some kind of problem."

"But what about the dogs?"

"Forget the dogs, Eyal." His brother eyed him. "Tomorrow, if she doesn't move you forward, you ask to speak to her supervisor."

"I'm not very good at threats." He sipped the beer. "It might backfire."

"It isn't a threat," his brother told him. "It's a request."

"Oh."

His brother frowned for a few seconds. "No, you know what? Even better: don't wait for her to call you. There are other offices in that waiting area, right? Other doors?"

"I haven't seen any other doors open," Eyal told him.

"But there *are* other doors."

"Yes."

189

"Are there security officers in the room? Police?" His brother was smiling.

"Not really." Eyal tried to remember. "One at the entrance. And then, you know, all the cameras. And the dogs," he added, but so quietly that his brother couldn't hear him.

"Good. Then you can play stupid if it doesn't work out." His smile became a grin. "Easy for you, right?"

"Thanks."

"Once you've cleared the barriers, you keeping on walking straight through the room, open one of the other doors—not the crazy lady's—and you sit at the desk you find inside." His brother was laughing. "I do this all the time with clerks, Eyal. If anyone asks, you tell them that you've made a mistake. You apologize and go back out to the waiting room."

"Okay." Eyal wasn't following, but he was willing to try whatever strategy his brother suggested.

"But they won't ask," his brother emphasized. "Clerks never do. All day long, all they do is process paperwork. They've got no idea who's sitting across from them. You could be a guineafowl for all they care. You walk inside with confidence, and they'll assume that you're their next appointment. They'll process whatever you give them."

Eyal nodded. He wasn't relishing the notion of breaking the rules, but at this point, he'd try anything to end the repetitious exchanges the woman with the cards had initiated. It was worth a try. And his brother did have more experience in these matters than Eyal himself had. Slowly, he nodded a second time.

And then: "but what about the dogs?"

"Forget the fucking dogs, Eyal."

Eyal wished that he could forget them. But day and night—seeping even into his dreams now—the dogs followed him. Insistent and threatening. Central figures in the misery of the process he was enduring, even if his brother failed to understand it.

Too sane, Eyal supposed. His brother had always been too sane. And why the Consulate had sent the invitation to him, Eyal, rather than to his brother he'd never, ever understand—

"You're right." Eyal broke off his musing. "Sorry." He stood. "I'm going to sleep."

"You watch," his brother told him. "Tomorrow you'll put that bitch in her place."

Eyal shivered at the turn of phrase. But he didn't speak. Instead, taking up his stinking suit jacket, he wandered toward his bedroom. Hoping without a great deal of confidence that he'd be granted one night free of the oneiric dogs.

The next day, he spent only an hour and a half waiting behind the crowd-control barriers. The dogs prowling. One nipping at his heels as he showed his identification to the first of the security guards. Eyal decided to interpret the comparatively short wait as a good omen. And as much as he could, he ignored the dogs.

Thus, when he entered the waiting room, he did so with more confidence than he'd expected to bring with him. And rather than sitting in one of the plastic chairs and furtively selecting a likely target from among the closed doors, he walked, his head held high, toward a door embedded in the middle of the far wall—a few inches taller than the others, directly across from the entrance. A door that had intrigued him since his first visit.

On his way, he attempted to kick a skulking black Doberman out of his path, but he missed the thing, and his foot slid through air, momentarily unbalancing him. But he kept from toppling over. And, in any case, none of the other waiting applicants noticed his behavior any more than they ever did. Sheepish, he made sure of it.

When he reached the door, however, he didn't pause. Still riding on his confidence, he pulled his papers from the inside pocket of his suit jacket with a flourish, turned the knob, and stepped with determination into the room. His only fear was that the office would be empty. Uncertain as to how he would attempt a second room while still claiming ignorance or misinformation.

But the office wasn't empty. And Eyal was pleased by his luck for perhaps a half second or more. It wasn't, he told himself, empty. That was good.

Upon realizing what the room did contain, however, he forgot his optimism, set aside his confidence, and felt nothing but his chest clenching and his palms breaking out into a sweat. His heart beating ragged and painful. The black edges of incipient unconsciousness.

Fifteen or sixteen women, he finally allowed himself to see, were ranged about the place in myriad, unusual positions. Sitting. Standing. Reclined. Some on chairs. Some on the desk itself. Many on the floor. Not at all what one would have expected of clerks. And all, at present, were staring at him, Eyal. All having been interrupted in the midst of doing—things—that Eyal wouldn't have believed possible had he not witnessed it. Even on the websites his brother frequented. All naked.

The woman with the cards was there. Though, obviously, missing her beige or grey or cream suit. As was the woman Eyal knew instinctively must be The Virgin. Though not looking all that virginal, as far as Eyal was concerned.

Taller than the others, her skin was so pale that it was transparent. Eyal could see every one of her blue veins, from those in her temples to those in her wrists to those, well, in other places. Her hair was sharp. Her bones were sharp. Everything about her was sharp. Except for her eyes—which were icy instead. Boring into his own. Her fingers were in places that made Eyal, despite his terror, blush.

But Eyal didn't apologize. Nor did he back up and close the door. He couldn't. He simply stared at them. Unable to move. To speak. Even his brother, a useless part of his mind prattled at him, wouldn't have known how to react to this situation. There was a limit to suavity.

"Not one word," The Virgin finally said to him after over a minute of immobility. "Not one single word."

"I—" he began.

"That was a word."

And Eyal, suddenly free to move, twisted back to the sound of a baying howl. Followed by another. And another. And a fourth.

In the doorway stood both the Doberman and the Mastiff, their lips pulled back, growling and slavering at him. Behind him Eyal could feel the breath of something else. Large and closing. When invisible teeth sliced through his calf, ripping his dress trousers, however, he stopped analyzing the situation. He knew, primitively and reflexively, that he must run.

Already bleeding from the chunk that whatever it was had torn from his leg, Eyal leapt over the two dogs blocking the door—momentarily surprised by an agility he didn't know he possessed—and skidded into the waiting room. Though nimble, his feet felt slippery. Clattering and ungainly on the smooth floor in a way that he didn't understand, but also didn't take the time to examine.

He did, though, notice as he bounded through the exit and toward the central parts of the fortress, that the seats along the wall of the waiting room were empty at the moment. Or, not empty. In place of the six or seven applicants he'd remembered earlier, Eyal saw six or seven small stone statuettes. Also waiting. Human-like even in their alien morphology. Not human enough, unfortunately, to help him.

As the dogs chased him, hard on his tail but not—once again, to his surprise—gaining on him, Eyal decided to force his way through the main entrance of the Consulate and into the restricted sectors of the building. Someone there would pull the dogs off of him. One of the Marines, at the very least. And surely they'd understand his decision to violate their cordon given his current circumstances. The limits to security echoing, he felt, the limits to suavity.

The area outside the entryway was also empty, however. And as Eyal passed a sculpture of Our Great Founder shaking hands with a frail woman in a wig and buckled heels, he saw nothing but additional carved rock figurines. Strewn about the base of the statue. Along with a several packages of facial tissue and three or four toothbrushes that Eyal wouldn't have touched with a stick. A few of the rocks appeared to have been frozen in the act of approaching the door.

Eyal paid them little attention. Though he managed to get himself into the lobby of the building, the time he spent fumbling at the door—his hands refusing to respond to the signals his brain was sending to them—allowed the dogs nearly to catch up to him. And as he skittered into the

multistorey gallery, he felt teeth slashing into his
upper left arm.

Letting out a non-human scream of pain,
he sprinted forward, unthinking, and found
himself in some sort of restaurant or cafeteria.
Numerous little round tables. Food cooling on
counters. Blueberry muffins. But no people.
Nothing but the rocks. Rolling here and there on
the floor. A few propped up in the seats. Nothing
sentient.

Before the dogs could corner him, Eyal
made his way down a flight of concrete steps. Past
an empty shooting range, two rocks and a package
of golden ammunition spilled on the floor. From
there, he managed to infiltrate a sizable kitchen,
slamming the door behind him on a drooling set
of fangs that seconds before had nipped off the tips
of two of his fingers.

Or, he thought they were fingers. They had
once been fingers. The bruised mash that was left
behind looked to Eyal like nothing human at all.
Holding and cradling his hand, he stared about
him. No one in the kitchen. Nothing but a smear
of blood across a cutting board. He didn't like the
look of the blood. And the dogs had already
broken through the door he'd halfheartedly
blocked.

Pushing his way into a labyrinthine set of
stairways and narrow corridors that he assumed
constituted some sort of fire escape, Eyal
attempted to lose the dogs by doubling and tripling
back on his mazelike path. Though he did confuse

himself almost fatally, however, the dogs had little difficulty keeping to his trail. One snapped at his face and tore through his cheek, just as Eyal stumbled into a vast, dim expanse of cubicles and screens.

No one was there. Many of the chairs were occupied by the little rocks. A few were tilted over on the keyboards. And one was clogging a coffeepot that was still sluggishly producing brackish liquid. But Eyal saw nothing living. Nothing but the dogs, which had spread out across the field of cubicles in a wolf-like formation. Baying at and stalking him.

He twisted back and found another set of stairs. Ran up and up, panting and slipping, until he could run no longer. The top floor. When he stepped out of the stairwell, he saw that the entire corridor was filled with rocks. So packed together were they that with his uncomfortably contracted feet Eyal had difficulty picking his way across them. But a distant sound forced him forward. A lifesaving sound. The sound of a human voice. A human conversation.

The door to the large office at the end of the corridor, the source of the voice, stood open. Breathing heavily, Eyal staggered into the room. Then he collapsed and lay sweating and bleeding on the floor.

Looking up, he saw a young man sitting behind a large desk. Upstanding. Average-looking. Not the Consul General, whose photograph Eyal had seen in the waiting area at Visa Services. The man was babbling lovingly to a rock that he supported with two hands before his face.

"Please," Eyal said to the young man. "Help me."

The man continued to croon to the rock. Ignoring Eyal. Ignoring the sound of the dogs converging on the room.

"Please," Eyal repeated.

In terror, he stopped speaking. The Mastiff and the Doberman had loped into the room. Followed by the remainder of the pack. Growling, pacing back and forth in front of their prey, they drew closer. Eyal wished that he could close his eyes, but he couldn't get the signal from his brain to his face any more than he'd been able to control his hands before.

After fifteen or twenty seconds of circling, the Doberman sprang forward and stripped a piece of flesh from his shoulder. Playing with him. Detaching a smaller chunk from the bleeding meat that it had secured, the dog backed a half a foot away and began gnawing at its prize, its teeth and lips streaked with red. The signal for the remainder of the pack to finish the job.

As the Mastiff ripped through his throat and the other dogs began worrying at his stomach and upper legs, Eyal's eyes wandered up to the window above him. And just before the world went black, he noticed that the rocks, lined up side by side on the windowsill, were looking down on him, watching his fate. Alien and curious.

198

One, Eyal thought as his spine cracked and his lower body went mercifully numb, was holding a clipboard. One held a small, stone visa. And one, to his delight, looked remarkably like his older brother.

But after that, Eyal had difficulty identifying them. As The Virgin's dogs completed their task, and as the young man continued, endlessly, to speak with the rock he held in his hands. In love.

The End

Also From Tiny Boar Books

On the Nature of Things
by T. Edward Abbott

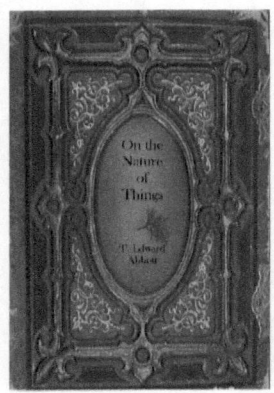

Welcome to the troubled town of Y—ce, where mud and spider silk, bryophytes and hedgehogs' quills have taken on lives of their own.

Things haven't been the same in the village of Y—ce since the forest encroached. A beautiful boy and his sister have developed a taste for wood and eaten their mother's house. The local brewer has purchased a tanned leather sculpture of a disagreeable girl affixed by her feet to a loaf of bread. A cat with reconstructed footpads has transformed an unemployed woman's prospects, though perhaps not in the manner she would have chosen. And an aging widower has found himself bound, literally, to the red lady's slipper orchids he planted over his dead wife's grave...

Evoking Robert Aickman and Neil Gaiman at their sinister best, these interlocking stories of obsession and anxiety, of the uncanny and the illusory, transform the daylight realm of the fairy tale into a murky underworld of horror. As eerie as it is immaculately realized, *On the Nature of Things* is a magical portrait of The Wood in its stripped, unadulterated form.

The Crow Foretells a Stormy Day
by T. Edward Abbott

Take care when you visit the city of A—che, where the ice and the frost, the sunlight and the spring melt have their own ideas about the meaning of sustainability.

No one lives in the city of A—che for the climate. When it isn't grey, dim, mildewed, and miserable, it's sweltering, smoldering, and oppressive. And that was before the weather began to act up. Since then, little has gone as it should. The small footprint left by an eco-entrepreneur has melted away altogether. The car wash patronized by the manager of a construction site has involved itself in an unusually authentic solstice celebration. An eccentric choreographer who likes to throw axes at his dancers has given his newest ingenue a breakthrough role that, quite literally, sets fire to the house. And a celebrated conceptual artist has found his muse in a blind and needy sea serpent...

Vivid, literate, and darkly comic, *The Crow Foretells a Stormy Day* is a masterwork of precision horror. If Walter de la Mare or China Miéville collaborated with Edward Gorey, the world they imagined might read something like this.

The Thirteen Trials of Dr. Marion Bailey
by Felicity St. John

Scholar, spy, and Gothic heroine…Marion Bailey reads like Iris Murdoch or Muriel Spark re-inventing Indiana Jones and George Smiley.

Dr. Marion Bailey has had a checkered career, from the moment she washed up in 1927, a failed scholar blindsided by the brutality of the British Mandate in Iraq to her final adventure in 1938, persecuted by a demonic gibbon conjured up out of a medieval Arabic bestiary. But throughout her tribulations, she's dragged along with her the same traits and wounds: a tortured genius for decoding obscure dead languages, a fragile psyche increasingly battered by each of her exploits, and a tormented responsiveness to the medieval detritus churned up in her wake—and then gobbled up by the British Museum.

Now, in 1967, her forty-year-old son has discovered among this detritus—the five-hundred-year-old Ottoman Book of Kings, the eleventh-century Fatimid pearl of enormous size, the thirteenth-century Ilkhanid celestial globe, and the amorous golem cobbled together by an illegitimate French Queen and a Nabatean magician of ill repute—a manuscript that even his mother refused to touch. As he decides whether to take up the silent challenge posed by the sealed book, he slips backward in time, appraising, finally, his mother's troubled history.

A House in Fragments
by E.M. Hakewessell

A fever dream, a comedy, and an unsentimental portrait of madness, magic, and brilliance, A House in Fragments explores a doomed romance between two pathologically detached people.

High on an island hilltop sits a wood and glass fortress. Built for a genius, it once dominated the surrounding population, human and otherwise. Now an object of ridicule, it houses a lonely recluse barricaded in an attic, terrorized by the possibility of contact with the world. He ventures out only at night to collect stray bits of moss and lichen for what he believes is his art.

Or is it a house at all? To the inhabitants of the island's east shore, it's a driftwood hut. A ruin. Sheltering a hermit in which they only half believe. A madman invented by estate agents out to explain why no one climbs to the invisible summit. Uncongenial to development.

Or perhaps it is neither of those. When a series of inexplicable weather events forces the hermit and a troubled resident of the east shore onto a collision course with one another, both begin to wonder.

A haunting portrayal of what may or may not be mental illness, what may or may not be the thin space between incompatible worlds, *A House in Fragments* is also a story of the marvelous that permeates everyday life—and of the crossing points that sane people dismiss as a trick of the mind.

There's also a petulant faun.

www.ingramcontent.com/pod-product-compliance
Lightning Source LLC
Chambersburg PA
CBHW022058170626
46808CB00002B/496